Palo Alto City Library

The individual borrower is responsible for all library material borrowed on his or her card.

Charges as determined by the CITY OF PALO ALTO will be assessed for each overdue item.

Damaged or non-returned property will be billed to the individual borrower by the CITY OF PALO ALTO.

P.O. Box 10250, Palo Alto, CA 94303

GAYLORD

HALFHYDE OUTWARD BOUND

Halfhyde novels by Philip McCutchan:
Beware, Beware the Bight of Benin
Halfhyde's Island
The Guns of Arrest
Halfhyde to the Narrows
Halfhyde for the Queen
Halfhyde Ordered South
Halfhyde and the Flag Captain
Halfhyde on Zanatu

Other novels by Philip McCutchan:
Cameron in the Gap
Orders for Cameron
Cameron in Command

HALFHYDE OUTWARD BOUND

Philip McCutchan

St. Martin's Press
New York

HALFHYDE OUTWARD BOUND. Copyright © 1983 by Philip McCutchan. All
rights reserved. Printed in the United States of America. No part of this
book may be used or reproduced in any manner whatsoever without
written permission except in the case of brief quotations embodied in
critical articles or reviews. For information, address St. Martin's Press,
175 Fifth Avenue, New York, N.Y. 10010.

Library of Congress Cataloging in Publication Data

McCutchan, Philip, 1920-
  Halfhyde outward bound.

  1. Great Britain—History, Naval—Fiction. I. Title.
PR6063.A167H35 1984   823'.914   83-27259
ISBN 0-312-35691-9

First Published in Great Britain in 1983 by George Weidenfeld & Nicolson
Limited

First U.S. Edition

10 9 8 7 6 5 4 3 2 1

HALFHYDE OUTWARD BOUND

ONE

St Vincent Halfhyde came awake, slowly and painfully. His mouth was like the bottom of a parrot's cage, filled with the gritty feel of sawdust, and his head rang like a ship's bell. On the floor above, a cat sounded as though it was stamping its feet. The smallest sound went through Halfhyde like the jab of a marline spike. He retched violently and broke out into a cold sweat as the sleazy room swayed around him. His recollections of the night before were so hazy as to be virtually non-existent. He remembered falling in with a seasoned shipmaster, a short man in a tall hat who had been having his final fling ashore before taking his windjammer out of the Mersey and south for Cape Horn. Sobriety had lain ahead and Captain McRafferty was making hay while he could, and had drawn Halfhyde with him in his almighty haywain . . .

Liverpool was a roistering hell of a place. As the nineteenth century moved towards its end and the old Queen grew even older and more revered and the Prince of Wales waited impatiently for his inheritance and his freedom, Liverpool was reaching a peak of prosperity, its docks and wharves crowded with masts and spars, with bales of cargo to and from all the world's ports, with swearing, blaspheming, hard-living and hard-drinking stevedores and ships' officers and crews, the latter having largely come through purgatory to the Mersey and soon to be off again for another dose.

It was no wonder the public-houses did a roaring trade in whisky, gin and beer. One of the best and busiest was the Bear's Paw, handy for the docks on the Birkenhead side of the river. It had been in the Bear's Paw that Halfhyde had made the casual acquaintance of Captain McRafferty. 'I am being driven to the drink,' Captain McRafferty had said as he emptied his seventh glass of Dunville's whisky, 'against my will.'

'Indeed?'

' 'Tis the truth I'm telling you, my friend. 'Tis the filth and smoke that's doing it.' McRafferty waved an arm towards the vicinity of the river. 'All those dirty steamers that send their stink to heaven to offend the good Lord's nostrils. There's more and more of them today, driving sail from all the seas.' He laid down half a sovereign on the bar, and signalled up his eighth Irish whisky. He gathered up nine shillings and eightpence change in silver and copper. This he thrust into a leather purse; Halfhyde regarded the purse sardonically: a purse was the symbol of a mean man, and McRafferty hadn't bought him so much as one drink, a compliment that he had not hesitated to return. Each paid for his own. 'There's a new breed come in with the steamers,' McRafferty went on, not in the least discommoded by the amount of drink he had taken. 'Engineers, they call themselves, and think they should be classed as officers so I'm told. They're black with filth, with oil and grease and coal-dust. It would not be possible to have them in any decent ship's saloon. Now I'll tell you something.'

'Yes, Captain?'

'Never would I take a steamer to sea. I'd sink first. I'm a sailing-ship man and always will be. And you?'

Halfhyde smiled. 'Steam has been my own experience, but —'

'I might have known it,' McRafferty said in disgust. 'You look like a seaman and yet you don't – that's steam for you! When I was young ships were made of wood, the men who sailed them were made of iron. Now it's the other way round, so help me God. Iron ships and wooden men. Drink up and maybe I'll stand you the next.'

Halfhyde gave a hiccup. 'You don't really mean that, Captain.'

'Well now, maybe I don't. You have money?'

'Enough for my humble needs.'

'Then I don't mean it. Drink up just the same. What's your ship?'

'At this moment, I have no ship. That's to say —'

'On the beach. I see. Your line, man?'

Halfhyde said, 'Grey Funnel.'

'Grey Funnel?'

'Her Majesty's Navy, Captain. But I have a sabbatical. I have recently been placed, not for the first time, upon the half-pay list.'

'You mean,' McRafferty said with much deliberation, 'You have been booted out. I like an *honest* man, not one who uses euphemisms.'

'I am no liar, Captain McRafferty,' Halfhyde said. He set his glass down hard enough to break it. Whisky and blood stained the bar. 'I told you I am on half pay and that's the truth. If —'

'Very well, I accept your word. It is not important to me after all,' McRafferty said off-handedly. 'And now? Have you come to Liverpool to look for more active employment aboard a ship, or what? Are you in need of further pay, and have found that no one ashore stands in need of those trained to the sea?'

Halfhyde said, 'I wish to return to sea, certainly. But I'm not in need of a permanent berth. I intend sailing ultimately as an independent shipmaster.'

McRafferty gave a loud laugh followed by a belch. 'Your pardon. Damme, you're mad! You sound like an owner, as I also —'

'That's what I intend to be after acquiring some experience aboard a merchant ship,' Halfhyde said. 'Then I shall be in the market for a small but well-found ship, and it must be steam.'

* * *

Coming dizzily that next morning through the fumes of Dunville's, Halfhyde knew that he was not in his customary lodging but had no idea where he might be. No matter; he was alive and uninjured by the gangs of evil-minded men who roamed the night streets and alleys of Liverpool. He racked his brains in an attempt to remember exactly what he had told

3

Captain McRafferty. One thing he was able to recall: McRafferty had asked him to go aboard his ship, the fully rigged *Aysgarth Falls* of which he was owner as well as master. A time had been set for noon. Halfhyde, whose family farmed a large area of Wensleydale in Yorkshire not far from Aysgarth falls, had no difficulty in remembering that name. There had been a bargain in the air: McRafferty had seemed interested in taking him to sea for a consideration, but in what capacity now eluded Halfhyde's memory. The night had turned into a debauch and at last Captain McRafferty had departed, still upright, to seek out female company for what remained of the hours to daylight. Halfhyde had left the Bear's Paw and called a cab; in the cab he had passed out. The cabby, by a stroke of luck a decent man, had driven him behind a decrepit horse to a respectable lodging-house, one where his drunken fare would not be shanghaied to sea and the uttermost ends of the earth by a boarding-house master. The cabby had recompensed himself for his thoughtfulness by delving into Halfhyde's pockets and extracting two golden sovereigns, enough for a month's food for himself and his horse. Halfhyde had no female company, though he could well have done with some . . . as thoughts of Captain McRafferty receded they were replaced by thoughts of the erstwhile Miss Mildred Willard, now his wife by unkind fate. Halfhyde had spent some of his naval career in avoiding Miss Willard, daughter of a vice-admiral, from Hong Kong to Malta. When as lieutenant-in-command he had brought the torpedo-boat destroyer *Talisman* into Portsmouth dockyard from the South Pacific to face an Admiralty enquiry into the death of Captain Watkiss in distant waters, he had found Vice-Admiral Sir John and Lady Willard ensconced in their retirement in a splendid house in the High Street of Old Portsmouth, not far from the George Hotel where Lord Nelson had passed his last night before sailing to the glory of Trafalgar. Having met the admiral and his lady at a reception, Halfhyde had been bidden to dine at the house and had renewed his acquaintance with Miss Mildred, who was still unmarried and likely, it had seemed then, to remain so . . .

Halfhyde had had her photograph pressed upon him before

he had come north to Liverpool and it was in his baggage at his proper lodging; he grimaced at the thought of it. Mildred was ill-favoured as to face and figure, closely resembling the horses that were her life's interest. All her talk was of the Row in Hyde Park, of Ripon, of Newmarket and of little else except of course of the dear Queen. Her God was bloodstock ... Halfhyde savagely cursed the whisky bottle that had led him to a proposal, as much to stop the wagging of her tongue as anything else. As a man of some honour, he had felt unable to withdraw when sober. There was another aspect too: at that time unaware that he was to be placed on the half-pay list, as a result of censure in regard to the untimely death of the extraordinary Captain Watkiss, who in fact had virtually committed suicide by his remarkable behaviour towards the Japanese and Russians, Halfhyde had felt impelled to keep on the right side of Sir John Willard and no less of Her Ladyship, the admiral's personal prod.

The preliminaries leading to the wedding at St Thomas' church had been torture. A prospective son-in-law having been taken like a prize, Lady Willard had lost no time. Halfhyde was trapped like a man undergoing cell punishment in Detention Quarters. There had been one bright spot: Sir John's brother, Henry Willard, squire of a village in Hampshire. Hunting, shooting and fishing his interests might be; conventional – but Henry Willard was very human and detested his brother and sister-in-law. He and Halfhyde found much in common in that regard.

'Pompous bore,' Henry Willard remarked one day. 'Dreadful wife, just like a hen's backside – her mouth I'm referring to, my boy. Mildred's worse, though I shouldn't be saying this to her fiancé, of course. You'll forgive me?'

'Indeed I will, sir.'

Henry gave him a shrewd look. 'Well, now, that speaks volumes. You're being a bloody fool, y'know. Get out of it while you can.'

'I'm bespoke, sir —'

'Yes, yes, I know that. By God, you'll regret it! A breach of promise action's a better thing by far than a lifetime of regret,

Halfhyde.'

They were walking one of Henry Willard's fields. Halfhyde navigated round a cowpat. 'As a man of honour —'

'Oh, quite. I understand, naturally, and your attitude does you great credit, my boy. But as someone who seems about to become your uncle-in-law, if there's such a title – well, I'm entitled to speak my mind, I think – hey?'

'Certainly.'

'For the last time, then – after the marriage it'll become an impertinence and you'd be entitled to knock me down. But that girl has me beat. Even I can't stomach horse talk morning, noon and night, I realize there are other things in life. I dare say you do, too.'

'Yes, sir.'

'Then go and enjoy 'em while you can,' Uncle Henry said energetically, waving his walking-stick.

After Halfhyde's visit to the Admiralty the world had seemed a place of woe and gloom, the sunshine gone for at least a year. He had been interviewed by the Second Sea Lord himself, and that high-ranking officer had seemed disinclined ever to recommend Halfhyde for the full-pay list again. Too many times in the past he had proved, however efficient and loyal, to be a thorn in the sides of Their Lordships of the Admiralty. His habit of outspokenness was held against him; so was his habit of running counter to the orders of his seniors when he saw those orders as either ludicrous or downright dangerous. Halfhyde had never been tactful, had never been inclined to suffer fools, had never shrunk from a head-on collision with brass-bound authority; and he had suffered previous periods of unemployment on the half-pay list, residing in Camden Town with the good Mrs Mavitty, his landlady, his clothes growing seedier and more frayed, his footsteps taking him past the London clubs where ultimately he could no longer afford to repay hospitality and therefore refrained from entering. But this time there was to be no Mrs Mavitty. The Admiralty had taken their time in sending for him, and in the interval Lady Willard had seen to it that Halfhyde was wed, and he had endured a short honeymoon in Scotland, during which he had spent a day

6

propelling Mildred down Loch Lomond in a rowing boat and had been visited by strong desires to bundle her ashore on one of the small islands and leave her there for ever and a day. He it was who had insisted upon Scotland, and the highlands in particular, because, to his knowledge, there was no racecourse north of a line drawn from Glasgow to Edinburgh; the Scots, like himself, preferred whisky and the bagpipes. It was perhaps significant that there had never been more than one cavalry regiment of Scots in all Her Majesty's Army. Mildred it was who, denied such pleasures as she might have found in the horsey vicinities of Ayr and Paisley, Lanark and Edinburgh, had nagged continually about his choice and had grown more and more morose, pining for the saddle and the hunting field, and had bought every picture postcard she could find that depicted a horse and had stationed these around their hotel bedroom as her father might when serving have disposed pictures of his fleet. And at the end of the honeymoon month, Mildred was still a virgin. She had proved as determined as any well-bred horse at a jump.

Soon after their return to occupy, temporarily, four rooms in Admiral Willard's house, the Admiralty had demanded Half-hyde's presence and thereafter the atmosphere had grown cold: the Admiral didn't like a half-pay son-in-law and neither did his wife, who said so frequently.

It was this that had driven Halfhyde to his understanding mentor, Uncle Henry; and Uncle Henry, as generous as he was friendly, had provided a solution. Go back to sea, he had said, in the merchant ships. Buy yourself a small steamer, command it yourself, and range the world, leaving Mildred to her parents in the meantime.

Halfhyde had laughed at the idea. 'And the money to buy a ship, sir? Where in heaven's name does that come from? From my father-in-law, who might be glad enough to get rid of me at any price?'

'No. From me,' Henry Willard said. 'I can raise thirty thousand with no difficulty at all, and glad to. It'll be a loan, to be repaid when you're able. I see you making your fortune, my boy – and mine too, though I don't need it. I'll be a sleeping partner if you prefer it that way – an investment.' Uncle Henry had put a hand on Halfhyde's shoulder and looked into his eyes. 'I see honesty, reliability and independence of mind in your face, and the capacity for the command you've already held. Go to it with my blessing.'

* * *

Halfhyde had done so. His father-in-law had looked baffled when informed of his intentions, half glad, half peeved. He saw Halfhyde as a common seaman; but it was better than everlasting half-pay and a poverty-stricken presence around the High Street house. He had said it must be on Halfhyde's own head; he would know nothing about his son-in-law's movements if any enquiry should be made by the Admiralty – their Lordships would not approve of a half-pay officer being out of the country and employed other than in the naval service, and he would say nothing about it.

His arrangements made, Halfhyde went north by the train to Liverpool, with two purposes in mind: to bend an alert ear around the steamship market, and to make an attempt to get signed on aboard a merchantman so as to learn the handling of such at first hand as a preliminary step towards qualifying himself to take command of his own ship and to make her a commercial success from the start. Uncle Henry had insisted on his gaining that experience as a condition of the loan, and had not needed to insist far; Halfhyde was in full agreement. He needed to know the ways of the merchant ships even though, as a lieutenant of some years' seniority in Her Majesty's Fleet, he would be entitled, not to a certificate of competency as possessed by master mariners who had gone through the seven-year mill of sea-time and examinations, but to a certificate of service that would exempt him from the normal requirements of command. And he had determined to look for a berth aboard a windjammer, since it was the custom of steamship owners to demand sail experience of their masters, and Halfhyde would accept no less for himself insofar as he was able to do anything about it . . .

He stood up in the lodging-house bedroom. He swayed and felt sicker than ever; but he managed to stagger from the room to the landing, where he shouted for attention.

A stout woman clad in black emerged from a doorway in the narrow hall below. She called up, 'So you've recovered, 'ave yer? Lawks a-mussy, never did I see the like —'

'Rubbish,' Halfhyde snapped. 'Liverpool's not Cheltenham and well you know it. I require water – hot, with soap and a towel. And a razor, a clean one and sharp. I'd be obliged if you'd jump to it.'

There was no particular response from below. The woman was flummoxed. The voice was that of a gentleman and it held authority, the certainty of being obeyed without question. A short sound like 'Hah!' floated up to Halfhyde, followed by the banging of a door. Within ten minutes his requirements had been met. He rejected the offer of breakfast, asking only for very strong coffee.

* * *

'So you've come aboard,' Captain McRafferty said, sounding somewhat surprised. Halfhyde had been taken below to the saloon of the *Aysgarth Falls*. A young woman had been sitting at the long table, doing some crochet work – a pretty girl of Irish colouring, aged about twenty at a guess. Halfhyde had not been allowed to do more than wish her good morning before Captain McRafferty entered from his cabin and sent her packing. 'Men's business,' he said, and that was all he needed to say. The girl had gathered up her work and left them alone. The saloon was over-warm despite the cold of a bleak spring day; a fire glowed in the grate, the coals sputtering behind a guard.

McRafferty indicated a chair; Halfhyde sat. 'You've made up your mind?' McRafferty asked abruptly.

Halfhyde stroked his long chin; he was reluctant to confess to having failed to recall most of the previous night's talk. He fished. He said, 'Your offer was somewhat inconclusive, Captain.'

'It was not. On the contrary, it was definite. The truth is this:

9

you were too damned drunk to remember what the devil it was I said. You'll admit that now?'

Halfhyde grinned and said, 'Yes. I'm sorry.'

'You need not be. Many a good man gets drunk ashore. You'll be needing a hair of the dog I don't doubt.' McRafferty turned aside, opened a cupboard and brought out a bottle of Dunville's, two tumblers and a jug of water. He half filled each tumbler. 'Help yourself to water. I'll take mine neat.'

He did; he put the tumbler to his lips and appeared to suck it up in one long draught. He said, 'The bottle will not reappear after tomorrow morning until the ship berths in Iquique. There is no drinking at sea aboard my ship. Well? Last night I offered you two alternatives: I'll take you as a passenger, or I'll sign you on articles as an able seaman, not at the full rate of pay but at a nominal shilling a month. You'll work hard and repay me by being a cheap hand. I'm short of seamen, as the fo'c'sles of the old windjammers always are today – the men prefer the ease and softness of the steamers, bad cess to them! Your answer was that as a passenger you would twiddle your thumbs and waste your time. As a fo'c'sle hand, by God, you'd learn the ropes – literally! You told me you'd had experience of sail, but you did not specify what it was. 'Tis that I'd like to know now.'

Halfhyde felt the whisky glow in his veins, bringing back a touch of health. He said, 'The training ship *Britannia* gave me some basic sailing skills. Then I was in the sail training squadron as a midshipman, under the Earl of Clanwilliam.'

McRafferty laughed. 'Aye, the Earl o' Clanwilliam, no less. There are few earls in the merchant ships, Halfhyde. You will find life harder here.'

'Yet Lord Clanwilliam drove us hard.'

Here, this morning, aboard his ship, Captain McRafferty seemed a different man, a man standing where he was acknowledged as God. Smiling, he said, 'You will embark on the hardest life that providence ever put in the way of man, and you will ship with some hard shipmates. Rogues the lot of them, or mostly – but fine seamen – again, mostly. Every ship has its share of loafers, who are not signed on again once found out. My First Mate, Mr Bullock, is a hard case who's done time in the down-easters under the Yankee flag – ships that have always carried bullies as mates. If you ship under me, then you'll be driven harder and for longer than any lord would drive. I have given you fair warning. Do you accept?'

Halfhyde finished his whisky. 'I accept,' he said quietly.

'Very well, then. You will learn plenty, Halfhyde. But there is one thing above all that you must learn for your own sake to forget, and quickly, and that is this, that you've held command of your own. For my part, I shall make no mention to anyone of your past, or of your future hopes as an owner. I shall make it known, if I need to, that you have done naval service – it will be, or should be, clear to the hands that you're no greenhorn.' McRafferty paused and turned away to pace his cabin. When he spoke again he came close to Halfhyde and kept his voice low. He said, 'There is a reason why I have a need for you . . . why you can perhaps be useful to me.'

'Yes, Captain?'

McRafferty said, 'I told you last night, I own my ship, as you hope to own yours. Times are hard in sail today. The expenses mount continually and cargoes are not always easy to find. No cargoes, no money – no money, no ship. The *Aysgarth Falls* is my home. It is very worrying – the ship is heavily mortgaged. What I am driving at is this: after we discharge at Sydney, I have as yet no homeward cargo promised —'

'Is there not always plenty of wool for home?'

'No,' McRafferty said with a shrug, 'not always. Sail is being beaten to it by these damned steamers – it's true our rates are preferential, but we have not the speed. And always I am forced to cut my rates a little more to obtain the cargoes. I repeat, it is very worrying for a shipmaster who also owns his ship.' He paused, pulling at his bushy side-whiskers. 'I have had to provide an additional form of income, a kind of insurance, in case there is no homeward cargo. I have arranged to pick up a passenger in Iquique, our first port of call, in Chile. I am being paid a not inconsiderable sum to take this person to Sydney.'

Halfhyde raised an eyebrow, quizzically. 'A not inconsiderable sum . . . do you mean a sum beyond what you'd normally expect?'

McRafferty nodded. 'You are quick enough to guess. Yes, that is the case.'

Halfhyde asked directly, 'Why are you telling me this, Captain?'

McRafferty shrugged and said simply, 'Because I trust you. You have an honest look, an honest way of speaking. I have had much experience of men, as all shipmasters have. I know a good man from a bad one. And as I've said already, I may need your help. Your advice.'

'My advice? I have no commercial experience as yet, and a passenger, I would take it, is a commercial proposition. Is not your First Mate the man for this?'

'It was my First Mate who arranged this passage, Halfhyde. A personal contact . . . a friend of a friend of a friend. I don't like it, but was forced by necessity to agree.'

'And your reason for not liking it?'

Captain McRafferty moved even closer and his next words were said almost into Halfhyde's ear. He believed his forth-coming passenger to be a man on the run, whether from the law or not he was unable to say. He admitted his suspicions to be based upon nothing more substantial than his instinct, but made reference to a long seafaring experience and a nose for trouble. He said, 'I would like to feel that I have aboard someone who has held – still holds – the Queen's commission. At a time of difficulty . . . I shall say no more for now, but possibly you will understand.' His tone changed and he moved away, becoming formal. He went on, 'The *Aysgarth Falls* leaves for Sydney on the tide tomorrow with a cargo of cased machinery and machine parts. After rounding the Horn we steer north for Iquique to take on a part cargo of nitrates, also for Sydney. You will report to the shipping office to be signed on articles in my presence by the Board of Trade's shipping master at two bells tomorrow forenoon.'

As he left the ship Halfhyde pondered McRafferty's words about his passenger and the help that might be required. Halfhyde was not sure that he entirely understood what McRafferty might be after, but one thing appeared certain. McRafferty did not trust his First Mate.

TWO

Once again wearing his tall hat, Captain McRafferty attended next morning at the shipping office to sign Halfhyde on articles, along with two other fo'c'sle hands neither of whom was sober. Making his way afterwards to the *Aysgarth Falls* with these two men, who had the aspect of men recently out of gaol, Halfhyde reflected on his wife, smug and snobbish in Portsmouth. During the afternoon she would doubtless be off on a round of visiting with Lady Willard, leaving cards on such socially possible persons as had recently moved to the naval town. Halfhyde's lips twisted in a smile as he recalled something Vice-Admiral Sir John Willard had said a few years ago in Malta, when Halfhyde had been bidden from his ship to the Admiral's residence for dinner. Sir John had commented upon his Flag Lieutenant's report of a probing visit to the wardroom of a torpedo-boat destroyer newly arrived on the Mediterranean station. *Socially quite impossible*, had been the Flag Lieutenant's edict, *not a gentleman among them*.

Sir John would spin into his grave if he could see his son-in-law now.

Halfhyde elicited that his new shipmates were named Float and Althwaite. Float had indeed come recently from gaol and was inclined to boast of it. 'Grievous bodily 'arm,' he said with relish, unasked. 'Best watch it, matey. Me, I don't like being crossed, all right?'

'All right indeed,' Halfhyde answered coolly, stepping across the filth and scum of the docks, avoiding bales of cargo, the wicked cargo hooks of the stevedores, and ships' mooring lines.

'I'm inclined to be the same myself, as a matter of fact, so don't cross me either – matey.'

Float gaped at him. Men didn't usually speak to him like that, having once been warned. He looked a shade unsure of himself; and the other man nudged him and said, 'Sounds like a gennelman, Float.'

' 'E'd best watch that and all,' Float said. Float was a thin man, but tough-looking. He reached into his clothing and showed the tip of a knife, making sure Halfhyde saw it. He said nothing, but the gesture was clear enough. The three men walked on, carrying their gear in canvas bags; Halfhyde had kitted himself out on leaving his lodging that morning, before reporting to the shipping office. His gear was simple: a couple of thick woollen jerseys, heavy duty trousers of coarse cloth, sea-boots, oilskin coat, sou'wester plus thick underwear, clasp-knife and lanyard together with personal necessities and toiletries: he had always shaved at sea and intended to continue doing so whatever the state of other chins; neither Float nor Althwaite appeared to have shaved for many days. The morning was foul with a penetrating drizzle, but Halfhyde walked jauntily and with a springy step. All new experiences were welcome to him and he looked forward with a sense of adventure. He and the others were met at the gangway of the *Aysgarth Falls* by a hefty man of about forty years of age sporting a drooping ginger moustache and a peaked cap. This man stood with his hands on thick hips, looking the three arrivals up and down.

'Names?' he demanded.

They gave them. The man said. 'I'm Mister Bullock, First Mate. You'll be getting to know that bloody fast. All right?'

'Yessir,' said Float and Althwaite together. They sounded sycophantic in Halfhyde's ears and no doubt in Bullock's, but he would be used to that. He told them to get for'ard and report for work on deck in ten minutes' time; Halfhyde was told to wait behind a moment.

Bullock said, 'The Captain's spoken to me about you. Done time in the Queen's ships, he said.'

'That's right, Mr Bullock.'

'Sir to the fo'c'scle scum.'

'Perhaps. But not to me – that is, not in the role of fo'c'sle scum.'

Bullock stared, fists clenching at his sides. 'Say that again.'

Halfhyde did so. Bullock's fists moved fast, but Halfhyde moved faster. He stepped neatly aside, and the First Mate's right fist crunched full into a heavy block on the mainmast shrouds. He swore, blasphemously, and made a dive for Halfhyde, who seized his wrists and held them fast.

Halfhyde said, 'I am not to be hazed by bullies, Mr Bullock, and I am not fo'c'sle scum, though some may be. That having been said, I know enough of the ways of the sea to understand that one's superior officers are normally addressed as sir. Now that we know where we stand, the sir you shall have.'

Halfhyde had an idea he was saved only by the appearance on deck of Captain McRafferty; but knew beyond a doubt that he had started off by making a dangerous enemy. In an ominously quiet voice Bullock ordered him for'ard. He obeyed. He went through the door beneath the break of the fo'c'sle into the space that was home to the twenty or so deckhands, a filthy compartment enveloped in a filthy smelly fug, its sides surrounded by tiered bunks which Halfhyde could only make out when his eyes had accustomed themselves to the gloom. The stench was appalling, a mixture of bilgewater and damp, of foetid human breath and sweat, of dirty clothing and bodies. Many of the hands lay on the bunks or on the deck, men recently returned from the shore, as drunk as lords and not yet fit to stir. Vomit lay around. A moment later the light filtering in from the door lessened and, turning, Halfhyde saw the threatening bulk of the First Mate. Bullock's voice cut like a knife through the murk of the fo'c'sle messroom, shouting the hands on deck and never mind the alcohol-drugged brains and limbs. As he left he made room for the ship's bosun, who started dragging the men out and dumping them on the deck, where the hoses were turned on them.

* * *

15

By sailing time it was a thoroughly wet day, with the Mersey rain teeming down in earnest; and the decks were still filthy, not yet cleared of shoreside grease and muck, the patina of Liverpool Town. Liverpool was a sailor's town, none quite like it anywhere else on God's earth. Solid and prosperous like the good old Queen herself, the buildings tall and imposing as they loomed over the crowded shipping in the port, worn with the soot and damp of Merseyside. And the smell: a smell made up of a magic mixture of mist and soot and tar laced with the fragrance of spices from the Orient, laced again with the smoke from the steamers so abominated by Captain McRafferty. But those steamers brought trade to the Mersey's acres of docks, its thirty-six miles of quays; the total tonnage, sail and steam, owned in Liverpool exceeded, as Halfhyde had learned, the tonnage of all the German Empire and amounted to three times the tonnage owned by all the United States of America. Halfhyde was glad enough to be a part of this challenging commerce, one of the cogs that would keep the wheels of Empire grinding on as much as had been the case when serving in Her Majesty's Fleet. Britain depended for her very survival on her seaborne trade, and thus upon her ships and the shellbacks who drove them through the storms of wind and water. These were the sinews of her being, of her current expansion into the greatest Empire the world had ever known. From Liverpool and other British ports her armies overseas in India and elsewhere were kept supplied and in good heart to fight the battles of the Queen-Empress who, from Windsor Castle, ruled a quarter of the world's inhabitants; the ships of England were the lifeline that kept an Empire and a way of life in being.

As sailing time approached, more drunken seamen drifted back aboard to be set to work immediately by the First Mate. Bullock sent his powerful voice for'ard from the poop to travel angrily along the wet deck and among the bleary-eyed seamen struggling through the haze of liquor to identify the myriad ropes, the braces and downhauls, the sheets and tacks, leechlines and buntlines. One man, the last aboard, brought his stomach up in vomit on the deck, and was seen by Bullock.

16

Bullock roard, 'O'Connor!'

The bosun turned. 'Aye, sir?'

'See to that man, and quickly.'

'Aye, sir,' the bosun said again, and moved for'ard. He laid hold of the offender and upended him, pushing the screaming face into the pool of vomit, rubbing it hard up and down the deck planking. Blood mingled with the vomit. The man started a dry retching; when he was allowed to stagger messily to his feet there was murder in his eyes; but the bosun gave him no chance before landing a heavy blow that put him down like a log. Then O'Connor swung round on Halfhyde, breathing heavily.

'Turn to, damn your eyes, and look busy,' he ordered. 'There's no skulking aboard a windjammer, not ever. Been to sea before, have you?'

'Yes,' Halfhyde said.

'Stand by to take the tug's line, then.'

Halfhyde looked away to starboard. From across the far side of the basin, a steam tug was to be seen approaching and as Halfhyde climbed to the fo'c'sle deck the tug used her steam whistle to give a monotonous blast of warning, a melancholy sound beneath the lowering, wet skies. Halfhyde reflected that this was to be a very different departure from that of a battleship or first-class cruiser leaving the south railway jetty in Portsmouth dockyard, with the guard and band of the Royal Marine Light Infantry paraded with its buglers to salute the Commander-in-Chief on proceeding outwards for a foreign commission.

* * *

Captain McRafferty climbed the ladder running up from outside the saloon through the hatch to the poop. Once again he was wearing his tall hat; but removed it as he went to the ship's side. Lifting it high, he cast it into the scummy water of the basin, then, dusting his hands together, turned away. Halfhyde had seen this performance from the fo'c'sle head; and made an enquiry of one of the apprentices, a youth who had

17

served two previous voyages under Captain McRafferty.

'Same each voyage,' the apprentice said, grinning. 'Buys a new one on each arrival home, chucks it into the basin on each departure.'

'For what reason?'

'He says it clears the mind of thoughts of the shore and is an excellent mental preparation for the voyage ahead.'

Halfhyde gave a shrug: ships' captains, be they Navy or Merchant Service, were often enough an enigma. He looked again towards the poop. Behind Captain McRafferty an officer of H.M. Customs and Excise had come up from below, one who according to the apprentice had examined the jerque note issued after the *Aysgarth Falls* had discharged her inward cargo and had been rummaged, and who had now cleared her once again for foreign. Behind this official came the mud pilot who would take the 2,000-ton windjammer off the berth and out through the locks, after which he would hand over to the river pilot.

The steam tug came up, fouling the day further with its black, smothering belch, coming through the grey overcast towards the outward bounder, ready to cut the last links with home. As she drifted up and lay off the bow, Captain McRafferty gave an ostentatious sniff and brought out a vast linen handkerchief which he held to his nose. There was a hail from her bridge, answered by the mud pilot who then lifted an eyebrow at the ship's Master.

McRafferty nodded in response then caught the eye of his First Mate. 'Single up, if you please, Mr Bullock.'

'Aye, aye, sir.' Bullock walked to the poop rail and shouted, 'Cast off the back-up headrope and sternrope, cast off breasts.' He turned to McRafferty. 'Springs, sir?'

'Let them go, Mr Bullock.'

Bullock shouted again. 'Let go springs fore and aft, stand by for'ard to take the line from the tug.' He made his way quickly along the deck to the bow. As the echoes of his strong voice died away there was a curious quietness, a quietness that Halfhyde recognized as the melancholy lull that always came before a ship proceeded to sea on a long foreign commission. He had known it when going China-side, or when leaving Portsmouth or Devonport yards to join the Mediterranean Squadron, or to take a ship to the far distant South Pacific. Halfhyde watched as the hands under the Second Mate, Mr Patience, bent to the spring leading aft from for'ard and heaved it in. There was a splash as the shore gang let go the sternrope from its bollard and the eye slid from the dockside into the murky basin water. The ship's crew brought it in, hand over hand, dripping, and coiled it down on the deck. With only one headrope and one sternrope to hold her now, the *Aysgarth Falls* waited for the order that would let the last lines go. The helmsman, standing stolidly behind the wheel on the poop, awaiting the Master's orders, chewed on a plug of tobacco, the dark juice running from the corners of his mouth while he kept an eye lifting on the masts now crossed with their yards – kept an eye lifting from sheer force of habit at this stage, for until the great sails were loosed there was little point in looking aloft and watching for the tremor that would indicate he was too close to the wind. A few moments later a heaving-line was sent snaking through the air from the tug, to be caught in the eyes of the ship by a seaman who brought it through a fairlead to the bitts. Behind it came a heavier line, then finally the tow-rope proper, a twelve-inch hemp hawser sparkling with rain and basin water. When this had been made fast the paddle-wheels of the steam tug turned over and the ship was drawn to the locks, where the Customs officer and the mud pilot disembarked. Ten minutes later the *Aysgarth Falls* was away for Sydney, with no one to see her go bar a few circling seagulls crying eerily as they swooped upon the trucks of the masts or skimmed the water for garbage, and a disinterested watchman looking down from the after rails of a steamer in a nearby berth: even the Customs man had turned his back and was making a dash through the rain for the warehouse.

* * *

Halfhyde was there to learn: it seemed that his first lesson was to be in how to haze the apprentices. The hands were standing

19

by the tug's line, and the braces, the latter so that the yards could be hauled round in a trice once the sails had been shaken out, to take the fullest advantage of the first sniff of a breeze and so be able to dispense with the tug – but there was as yet no hint of a breeze and it was clearly going to be necessary to tow right out, perhaps even as far as the Skerries. The water was dead flat and oily-looking, pocked by the rain. One of the newly-joined apprentices, a somewhat oafish youth named Mainprice, decided this was an idle moment, and took the opportunity to rest his weary back against the fo'c'sle guardrail.

He was spotted by Bullock.

'Damn your eyes, boy,' came the sudden rasp of the First Mate's voice. 'You're here to work, not to dream of home. Do you understand me, God damn you, boy?'

'Yes, sir.' Pig-like eyes met the First Mate's. 'But there's nothing to do, is there?'

'*Nothing to do* you say, is it?' Bullock was scandalized. 'Nothing to do, aboard a sailing ship away down the river?'

'Well, sir —'

'Stand up straight when you speak to me, boy!'

Mainprice stood straight but now there was a sullen look in his face. Bullock said, 'Go to the half-deck this instant, Mainprice. Fetch your toothbrush.'

'What?' Mainprice appeared non-plussed.

'You heard me. Just go.' Bullock's fists clenched.

Mainprice went; he came back with the toothbrush. Still there was no wind. Bullock said, 'Good. Now, the starboard anchor's dirty. Isn't it?'

Mainprice went across to where the starboard anchor was catted outboard of the guardrail, secure to the clump cathead. He looked, turned, and said, 'I don't think so, sir. It looks quite clean to me.'

Bullock scowled. 'You say it's clean. I say it's dirty. Look again.'

Mainprice's eyes flickered around the fo'c'sle. No one said a word, but all the men were grinning. Mainprice took a deep breath and said, 'All right, s'r, it's dirty.'

'I'm glad you agree, boy So clean it. Scrub it. With the

20

toothbrush.'

Mainprice opened his mouth, saw the look on Bullock's face, and shut it again. With smouldering mutiny in every movement, he climbed over the rail, hung on with one hand, and began scrubbing with the other. Bullock watched him for a few moments, then turned to one of the older hands, a man with a brown, wizened face like a monkey and no teeth. He said, 'Finney, you'll give us a send-off. We'll have a capstan shanty – just while Mister Mainprice learns that when I say a thing's dirty it bloody well drips filth and corruption.'

'Yessir,' Finney said, and scurried down the fo'c'sle ladder. He was back within a couple of minutes carrying a fiddle, and he sat himself cross-legged on the capstan and drew a bow across the strings in a preliminary movement. He grinned, gums agape, at the First Mate.

'Play, then,' Bullock ordered. 'And all hands sing.'

All hands did. As Finney played they sang in strong voices that were accustomed to call across wide spaces and into the teeth of gales; and the finest voice of all, oddly, was that of Bullock, who sang in a full-throated bass that would have done credit to any professional singer. For the first time Halfhyde heard the words that ever after would stay in his memory, stay long after such shanties had become a thing of the romantic past, dead and buried and forgotten along with the grey ghosts of the legions of seafarers who had sung them in all the world's ports:

'And it's home, dearie, home! Oh, it's home I want to be,
My tops'ls are hoisted and I must out to sea;
For the oak, and the ash, and the bonnie birchen tree
They're all a-growing green in the North Countree . . .'

* * *

The *Aysgarth Falls* came up towards Point Lynas in Anglesey, standing well clear of the land. Here she found her wind. Captain McRafferty reacted to it on the instant and passed his orders for sail to be made and the tug to be cast off. Seamen swarmed up the ratlines and laid out along the yards; those

21

remaining on deck stood by the sheets and braces under Mr Bullock, who shouted Halfhyde aloft under the Second Mate, Mr Patience, a young man not long out of his apprenticeship. Patience sent Halfhyde to the foretop, from which he was to climb further and go out along the footrope of the fore topgallant yard. All sail was to be made to the royals. As the bosun sent some hands to haul out the clew of the maincourse, Halfhyde began climbing. He went nimbly up the foremast ratlines, disdained the lubber's hole which Bullock was clearly expecting him to use, reaching the foretop via the outward-leaning futtock shrouds. From there he climbed higher and stepped on to the swaying footrope hanging below the topgallant yard. The deck looked minute beneath him; he was not far short of a hundred and twenty feet up, and the thin footrope seemed but a poor, insubstantial thing to which to entrust any man's life. Working from bottom to top the sails were loosed and hauled out, then the yards were hoisted to their positions by the halliards. As the sails filled Captain McRafferty trimmed them to the wind, sending the apprentices to tail on to the lee mainbrace, with a turn around the drum of a rail winch, to haul the yard to the correct angle. It was efficiently and quickly done even though some of the hands were greenhorns and soon the *Aysgarth Falls* was moving ahead for the turn south into the Irish Sea, making some four knots through only slightly ruffled water. When all the gear had been overhauled and the decks cleared up, all hands were mustered aft for the watches to be picked. They were told off into two watches under the mates, port and starboard, with Bullock having first choice. This done the hands, except for the watch currently on deck, were dismissed to go below and eat a late dinner.

The meal, Halfhyde found, not unexpectedly, was as unappetising as their surroundings in the damp, creaking fo'c'sle: a porridgey mess called burgoo, washed down with strong tea. The complaints were many; a big man sitting next to Halfhyde said that Slushy, referring to the cook, would get a knife in the gut if he didn't quickly mend his ways. The man, who was addressed by his messmates as Shotgun, looked as if he meant it. Halfhyde didn't comment but was dragged into the conver-

22

sation when Shotgun elbowed him in the ribs and repeated his remark in a loud voice. 'I was talking to you. It's polite to give a bloody answer.'

Halfhyde detected an American accent. He said, 'I'm sorry. Perhaps Slushy hasn't got his galley organized yet.'

'Then he'd bloody well better.' Shotgun turned and stared at Halfhyde. 'Where you come from, eh? Been to sea before?'

'Yes.'

'Thought so. I see you use the futtock shrouds. What line?'

Halfhyde said, 'I was in the Royal Navy.'

'Queen's ships, eh. Then you got a thing or two to learn.'

'No doubt. You?'

Shotgun laughed. 'Me, I done a lot of things. Prospected for gold, lumberjack, cowhand on a ranch. Then I came to sea.'

'In a British ship?'

'Sure. Any objections?'

Halfhyde shrugged. 'None at all.' Shotgun didn't carry on the conversation; Halfhyde had a shrewd idea he'd got out of America one jump ahead of the law. Such men were not unusual in the fo'c'sles of the windjammers and there were probably others aboard the *Aysgarth Falls*. In the dim light from the lantern that hung smokily from a deckhead beam Halfhyde studied his companions. They were a strange mixture of seasoned sailormen and men of the same kidney as Shotgun, men who had drifted to sea rather than chosen it as an occupation, Halfhyde guessed. Some of them would prove to be no-hopers and wouldn't last; some might well desert on the Australian coast. Many of the eyes were watchful, suspicious that every man might be against them. Once again Halfhyde found himself thinking of Mildred: if she could see him now . . . Before joining the ship he had found time to write her a letter telling her that he was Australia bound; and another to Henry Willard with a similar content. He grinned to himself: the face of Vice-Admiral Sir John Willard would be frosty in the extreme when his letter to Mildred arrived in Portsmouth.

Shotgun began another conversation. 'The Old Man, he's as mean as a shark. Food's not all Slushy's fault. Owners, they're all the same. McRafferty owns this ship. Know what you're in for?'

'You tell me.'

'Okay. You're in for filthy rotten food and bloody little water to drink or wash in. The afterguard'll have what fresh vegetables there are, and they won't last long. We'll not re-provision before Iquique and by that time the water'll be foul, unless we catch any rainwater on deck.'

Halfhyde nodded non-committally. He was not going to admit to the fact that McRafferty had told him of his ownership; that would indicate too great a familiarity between himself and the Master and he would suffer for it, besides which McRafferty had wanted nothing of that sort to be known in the fo'c'sle. But that McRafferty was mean was not news either; in the Bear's Paw McRafferty had said that a shipmaster who was also his own owner could not afford high living. Money was not to be spent lavishly; owners were in the business to make a profit, which was not the case in the Navy, where the Queen was lavish enough and could afford to be. Halfhyde had remarked that the men must be kept happy, and that the best way for that was a full stomach. McRafferty's answer had been short: their stomachs were quite full enough. And a mean Irishman, especially over drink as Halfhyde also remembered from the Bear's Paw, was something of a rarity. Shotgun went on to say that the Old Man was mean with his daughter also, and that she needed to kick over the traces for her own good. He came the master and owner over her as much as over the hands and never allowed her any freedom. Last voyage, Shotgun said, the old bastard had taken his revolver to Patience and threatened to shoot him if he went too near the girl.

* * *

Late the following afternoon the *Aysgarth Falls* had passed the Tuskar Rocks and had altered course to starboard towards the Fastnet whence she would take her final departure from the United Kingdom to head down through the South Atlantic for the passage of the Horn. Bullock was on watch on the poop; and Captain McRafferty was pacing the deck and looking

24

anxiously from time to time at the glass: he had noted a fall in the barometric pressure, a slow but steady drop that confirmed the heavy weather on their track ahead that his seaman's eye had noted already in the cloud formation.

'I don't like it, Mr Bullock,' he said. 'Pass the word for all hands.'

Bullock raised a shout for the bosun and the watch below was turned out, grumbling, to prepare the *Aysgarth Falls* for dirty weather. Below decks, everything movable was doubly secured against the heave of wind and water. On the deck itself, all lashings were carefully examined and where necessary double-banked. Bullock, accompanied by the bosun, opened up the tween-deck hatches and carried out such inspection of the cargo and the shifting-boards as was possible. Aloft, the gear was overhauled for good measure – footropes, ratlines, one or two new buntlines and leechlines were rove. From the main yard, where he had been sent by the First Mate, Halfhyde looked down on the work proceeding on deck: all skylights were being battened down and secured with tarpaulins, and all inessential deckhouse doors were being caulked up to prevent any inrush of water if they should ship a heavy sea. Men stood by the halliards and braces as McRafferty, from the poop, ordered the royal yards to be sent down and the flying jib unbent. The Captain, Halfhyde saw, was watching the sails closely, and spoke now and again to the man at the wheel, occasionally lending a hand himself to bring the ship quickly to the shifts of wind, which was already beginning to become oddly erratic and in fact had decreased if anything in strength. When the blow came and the preparations on deck had been completed, an extra hand would be sent to the wheel to help hold it steady. Looking ahead in the fading light Halfhyde found the Atlantic flat but somehow threatening, like a bottomless, evil pool. He had seldom seen the sea like this in home waters. There was a bad sign insofar as the wind seemed to have gone almost altogether now; there was a slatting sound as limp canvas flapped back against the masts and yards, and a rattle of blocks as an occasional light gust shook through the ropes. The feeling of threat increased, and Halfhyde saw the

25

tension in the faces of the men alongside him on the yard as, to McRafferty's orders, the storm mainsail was sent up.

'The Old Man expects a real blow,' one of them said. 'It won't be just playing about, not tonight.' He looked aside at Halfhyde. 'Best watch it. There's a golden rule aboard the windjammers: one hand for the ship and one for yourself.'

Halfhyde smiled. 'Thank you for the warning,' he said. 'It's not my first time aloft, however, and I don't expect to die just yet!'

The last of the daylight was going now. Ahead, on the starboard bow, a long low line of black cloud had formed and above this, the colour seeming to rise out of it, the sky was green-shot and dangerous. As Halfhyde looked towards this great bank of cloud he saw a curious transformation of the sea's surface, a sort of ruffling movement that spread from ahead with extreme rapidity and came down towards the *Aysgarth Falls*. As Halfhyde looked aft in expectation of orders from McRafferty, he saw the daughter's head emerging from the poop hatch, which had not yet been battened down. Miss McRafferty – Halfhyde had never so much as heard her christian name mentioned – stepped across the poop to speak to her father, who was in fact too preoccupied with his ship to notice her sudden appearance. He had cupped his hands to call out to the First Mate, and Halfhyde heard his shout.

'Mr Bullock, we have the wind west-nor'-westerly. Take in —'

Very suddenly, the voice broke off. Something seemed to have gone badly wrong on the poop; the spanker boom had swung wildly across the deck, heavy, fast and lethal. Men were shouting, and when the boom went smartly back the other way Halfhyde saw that the Captain's daughter had gone. Then something in the water, no more than a break of spray in the near darkness, caught his eye and he was aware of the white face staring up and the mouth open, calling desperately.

With no hesitation, Halfhyde dived from the main yard.

THREE

Halfhyde went in cleanly, came up well clear of the ship's side. He dashed water from his eyes. From the poop someone had thrown a lifebelt; Halfhyde saw it bobbing about on the waves, already white-topped and breaking. There was no sign of the girl now. Aboard the ship, the First Mate was running to the lee skids to lend a hand with sending away the lifeboat; already the chain gripes had been freed. On the poop, Patience and two of the hands had managed to get a line over the end of the spanker boom – it had parted its 3½-inch hemp guy pendant – and the wild swinging was coming under control.

With strong strokes, Halfhyde swam for the lifebelt, reached it and got an arm through it. Then he saw the girl breaking surface not far away.

He went for her, fast.

The wind was gusting strongly now, hitting the *Aysgarth Falls* with hammer blows out of the darkness and laying her over to leeward. McRafferty had passed the order to back the topsails and take the way off; and the royals and topgallants were already furled along their yards. Even so, and though scarcely two minutes had passed since the girl had gone overboard, the ship was drawing away as Halfhyde reached the half-drowned figure, laid his hands on her roughly, and drew her close in an attempt to get the lifebelt over her head and shoulders. Like any person in danger of drowning, she struggled violently.

'Easy!' Halfhyde shouted. 'Relax, and leave yourself to me. You'll be all right now, I promise you.'

It was no use; the struggling continued. All Halfhyde could

27

do was to retain his own grip on the lifebelt and press the girl close to his body, pinning her arms. She was gasping like a landed fish and Halfhyde guessed she would have swallowed a good deal of seawater and would have doubtless drawn some into her lungs as well. Meanwhile the two of them were being hauled to the ship's side on the line attached to the lifebelt; Bullock was heaving away with the assistance of McRafferty and one of the seamen who had been helping to snatch in the spanker boom.

Within another minute or two they were alongside, surging up and down the iron hull of the windjammer. A heavier line was sent down quickly and Halfhyde slipped a bowline around the girl, grasping the line himself above her head. They were hauled up and assisted over the rail to the waist. For a moment McRafferty, who had come for'ard from the poop, held his daughter in his arms, then released her as the saloon steward came up to carry her below.

McRafferty seized Halfhyde's hand. 'That was a brave thing to do,' he said. 'Thank you. I shall not forget it.'

Halfhyde made a gesture of negation then said, 'Your daughter, sir. She has taken water for a certainty. It must be got out of her lungs.'

'The steward —'

'I know how to do it, sir. Leave her to me. Your steward will not have had my training.'

McRafferty met his eyes then nodded. 'Very well,' he said curtly. 'Do your best.' He turned away, making back for the poop ladder where his duty lay. Halfhyde lifted the girl, who seemed to him feather light, and with the steward in attendance carried her up the poop ladder behind her father, and then down through the hatch to the saloon. He laid her gently on the settee that ran below a line of ports, now with their deadlights clamped down hard. Stripping away the soaked clothing and working quickly, he leaned his weight on the palms of his hands and bore down on her chest. Behind him stood the steward, Goss, apparently acting as chaperone.

The treatment seemed to work; the seawater was expelled and some colour came back into the girl's face.

'Feeling better?' Halfhyde asked.

She nodded without speaking. She was shaking like a pendant in a gale of wind. He turned to the steward, his naval authority coming back almost unconsciously. He said, 'Blankets, and quickly.' He saw the hesitation in the man's manner: his nose had been put out of joint. Aboard a merchant ship, it was the steward who provided the first medical attention before handing over to the Master, the final arbiter on health and injury at sea. Beside which, Halfhyde was nothing but a fo'c'sle hand. Halfhyde said, 'Jump to it, Goss.'

Goss turned away, looking sullen. Halfhyde called after him, 'Bring brandy as well. Look sharp!'

Goss said, 'Now look. I'm not here to take orders from bloody deckhands —'

'You will take orders from me and like it. I said, look sharp.'

The eyes of the two men met. Goss couldn't long meet the stare; he turned away, muttering. Halfhyde knelt down by the girl's side. He took one of her hands in his, felt the coldness, tried to give it some of his own comparative warmth. Like the fo'c'sle, the saloon held a damp, cold fug; the fire, along with that in the galley, had been drawn as part of the precautions against the bad weather. In a voice only just audible, the girl said, 'Thank you for what you've done.'

'It was nothing. Only what any man would have done.'

'Only you did it.'

He grinned. 'We'll not quibble, Miss McRafferty.'

Nothing more was said; the girl, who from a sense of modesty had drawn her wet clothing back over her body, closed her eyes. She had a beaten look about her; she was pretty enough, and attractive enough to make Halfhyde's pulse beat a little faster as he looked at the outline of firm breasts beneath the wet chemise, but even when not recovering from a dousing he had noticed the strain in her face. Probably it was no easy thing to be McRafferty's daughter and to live the life that was hers aboard a ship at sea. She needed the company of other persons of her own age, both women and men, and needed not to have every man deflected in advance by a hard, self-protective father. That, however, was no business of Halfhyde's.

Goss came back with blankets and a bottle of brandy. He tucked the blankets over the girl, then turned to Halfhyde. 'Orders of the Master,' he said. 'Nothing's to be drunk at sea. It's your responsibility if you ignore that.'

Icily Halfhyde said, 'I do not propose to drink myself. The lady's in need. Pour a measure and I shall feed it to her.'

Lips pursed, Goss poured a little brandy into a tumbler. Halfhyde took it. 'Thank you,' he said. At that moment he felt a sickening lurch of the deck beneath his feet and a heavy clatter of gear overhead. He would be needed on deck. 'You'll stay here and see that Miss MacRafferty comes to no harm.'

* * *

With extreme suddenness the *Aysgarth Falls* had been struck by a wind of near hurricane force. Hastening on deck Halfhyde was despatched for'ard by Bullock to assist in getting the remainder of the headsails off her. The jibs and foretops'l stays'ls had been sent down already but by this time a good deal of damage had been done. The fore and main upper tops'ls had been blown clear from the boltropes and had whipped away in tatters into the night. The *Aysgarth Falls* was taking it green and heavy over the weather rails and was riding sluggishly, wallowing, the wash-ports about as much use as a punt's baler against the constant inrush. Halfhyde struggled along waist deep in swirling, foaming water, battered by a screaming wind that forced the breath from his lungs, half drowning him as he went right under at times, hanging on for his safety to the lifelines and waiting for the seas to drain away from above his head as half the North Atlantic, as it seemed, pounded aboard and fought to subdue the ship, to stop her dead in her tracks. Around him green hands did their best to identify the ropes in a spider's-web of sheets, braces, lifts and stays as the spindrift flew into their faces from the wave tops and the solid water knocked their feet from under them and the wind continued to give ear-splitting tongue like a spirit in fury.

Just before Halfhyde made the fo'c'sle-head the forecourse joined the upper tops'ls, ripping out from the cringles, hanging for a moment from the rovings and then whipping away out of sight with a great crack that sounded clear and alarming above the gale. Mr Patience, the Second Mate, was laying about him like a lunatic when Halfhyde reached him, driving the hands on to get off the canvas before the rest of it went.

Toil and sweat and breaking muscles did it: that, and time. Halfhyde, calling upon his experience under the Earl of Clanwilliam and his sail training squadron, felt as though he had used up the whole night to take in the fore lower tops'l alone by the time it was clewed up to windward, with the sail itself full of wind; lowered away the halliards and eased off the lee sheet, clewed the yard down and then hauled up on the lee clewline and the buntlines – all in that raving, screaming wind and the darkness, with the ship heeling over to such an extent that the men on the yards were swept viciously through an arc of some seventy degrees as they fought to keep their footing on the thin, swaying ropes. Even when that job had been done the ship didn't seem to have been eased very much. She lurched and laboured still, the topgallant and royal masts bending and whipping beneath the strain of the movement.

Halfhyde heard the shout from aft: 'Clew up for reefing, main lower tops'l . . . let go maincourse halliards!' It seemed as though McRafferty meant to ride it out from now on, with just enough sail to keep the *Aysgarth Falls* into the wind and sea. The Second Mate came for'ard while other men went to the halliards belayed to the pinrail. Patience leapt above the rushing water into the shrouds, racing his fo'c'sle hands to the main lower tops'l yard to take his place at the weather earring for the reefing operation. He was aloft quickly, seeing the yard well down in the lifts and then laying out to the weather yardarm; by the time the men were on the footrope he had the earring rove. He hauled it taut and made fast, and when the job was done in the teeth of the gale he shifted to take the bunt for furling the maincourse. The wind was starting to come abeam; they were not getting the sails off quickly enough despite the best efforts of all hands. Another heavy gust struck, pressed relentlessly against the ship, forcing her over and over until the lower yards on the lee side seemed scarcely to clear the foaming

31

water that surged up to them; the yards seemed to Halfhyde to form an up-and-down, almost vertical steel link between the sea and the desperate, dark, spray-filled sky. But, slowly, the *Aysgarth Falls* righted herself and once the canvas was off her she rode more easily under her close-reefed lower top'sls. The hands were set to work clearing up the mess and after this the word was passed for one watch to go below. The fo'c'sle hands went with soaked clothing to their straw palliases in their cramped mess, along the deck of which slopped a couple of inches of dirty water, evil smelling and forbidding. Halfhyde, from a long ingrained habit instilled by his days as lieutenant-in-command of Her Majesty's torpedo-boat destroyers, remained on deck, and was addressed by Captain McRafferty himself when the two were alone in the waist.

'A sorry mess,' McRafferty said. He listened for a moment to the sounds of the storm and the thump and rattle of the blocks. 'There'll be much work for the hands when it's blown itself out, Halfhyde. We must bend new sails and renew a number of ropes and there'll be more overhauling to be done.'

Halfhyde was not in the best of tempers, in no mood to accept the lowly status of the fo'c'sle. His response was caustic and insubordinate. 'One would have thought,' he said, 'that more such work should have been done before sailing.'

'You are an impertinent fellow, Halfhyde —'

'I have been told that before, sir. I tend to say what I think, however.' He gave an acid smile. 'At least you will find me honest!'

McRafferty didn't answer for some moments. Then he said grudgingly, 'I shall not fault you for that. But you must understand – and as an owner you *will* understand in due course – that running gear costs hard-earned money and everything must be made to play its full part before it is discarded. It is all a question of money in a hard commercial world.'

'A short-sighted policy in my view. Worn-out gear leads to men being lost.'

The Captain gave a short laugh. 'Lives are the cheapest of commodities in the sailing ships, as you'll learn.' He turned away and went aft to pace the poop, hands behind his back, his eye lifted constantly to his masts and yards. Halfhyde could appreciate his enforced frugality, if not to the point of risking men's lives. To drive a windjammer through the seas for long hauls was a hard business, and no doubt it tended to make a man hard. But things would go differently aboard his own ship; Halfhyde had no intention of burdening his conscience with avoidable death.

* * *

McRafferty's words were to prove prophetic, and quickly: Halfhyde learned the following afternoon that death at sea was accepted philosophically and that men could be covered for more easily and cheaply than a ripped-out maincourse. The wind had moderated considerably during the forenoon, leaving behind it a cold grey overcast and close horizons. After the men had had their midday meal the Captain ordered them aloft to shake out the topgallants'ls on the fore and main masts. A young seaman, who looked clumsy enough to Halfhyde, lost his footing below the fore topgallant yard and went crashing downward. As he fell he hit a man on the upper tops'l yard, and this man, who happened to be the Second Mate, also lost his balance. The first man went into the water on the flat of his back, Patience came down hard across the bulwarks, gave a wild shriek of agony and collapsed inboard. Men ran to pick him up while Bullock sent away the lee lifeboat to search for the first man, who meanwhile had disappeared. The lifeboat's crew failed to find him during an hour's search, after which time McRafferty ordered the boat to return to the davits for hoisting. In the meantime Patience had died. His back had been broken and there was nothing to be done about that: the Ship Captain's Medical Guide was not adequate to the task of repairing broken backs and Patience had died in sheer agony. As soon as the Captain had pronounced him dead the body was removed to the sailmaker's cubby-hole to be sewn into its canvas shroud for sea burial. That burial took place as soon as possible, for bodies aboard ships were unlucky things and sailormen were a superstitious breed. Once the service had been read by Captain McRafferty in the presence of the hands, and the body had been slid from a plank into the sea, the work of the ship went on as before. The bosun was sent for and informed that he had been promoted to the position of Uncertificated Acting Second Mate.

'There will be no extra pay, Mr O'Connor,' McRafferty said in Halfhyde's hearing. The bosun seemed not to be worried about that; the accolade of the 'Mister' in the Captain's mouth was good enough to be going on with. Halfhyde grinned sardonically. Mr Patience, out of sight now beneath the waves and dropping astern as the *Aysgarth Falls* proceeded away from England, was already becoming nothing but a memory and now Captain McRafferty had acquired a replacement Second Mate at the bargain price of a bosun's pay. Halfhyde thought that the saving should go a long way towards some new deck gear.

* * *

The days passed into weeks; after the gale had abated the *Aysgarth Falls* had picked up a fair wind from the north-east and had run with all sail set to the royals, making a fast passage down into the South Atlantic to the equator. Now she had met the doldrums, that area of light, changeable winds or, more often than not, of no wind at all.

This was one of the times of no wind, and Captain McRafferty was on deck, whistling vigorously. This was the first time Halfhyde had seen the old sailing-ship adage in action: McRafferty was whistling for a wind. The ship lay motionless beneath a hot sun; sail had been shifted, the oldest suit of canvas being sent aloft to slat monotonously against the masts. Miss McRafferty sat in a deck chair on the poop dressed in a kilted frock of a deep prune colour, a sunshade held over her dark hair. As he whistled, McRafferty paced the deck in front of her, having the aspect of a guard. The girl had quickly recovered from her ordeal and was in good health, but her spirits seemed as low as ever. Halfhyde was at the wheel, keeping a sharp eye lifted for the first sign of a wind, the ruffle on the water or the shaking of a sail that would tell McRafferty he must stand by to trim the yards to catch the smallest breath that would send the ship even a short distance on her way. Time was money. Every extra day spent away from England meant more wages for the crew and reduced the value of McRafferty's cargo contract. Too many days had been lost already in the doldrums.

Bullock came up from the saloon hatch and the Captain stopped his whistling.

'Good morning, sir,' Bullock said.

'Good morning, Mister. Walk for'ard with me for a moment. I wish to take a look at the anchors.'

The two men went down the ladder from the poop, paced slowly towards the fo'c'sle, conferring with heads close together. There was, Halfhyde knew, nothing about the anchors that needed examination: McRafferty wished for privacy in his conversation, and Halfhyde's guess was that the talk was about the passenger waiting in Iquique, the passenger acquired through Bullock's contacts. McRafferty had not spoken of the matter again to Halfhyde; he was possibly worried now in case the passenger should not wait for a delayed sailing ship and seek a steamer instead to take him to Sydney.

Halfhyde smiled at the girl in the deck chair: by this time he knew her name to be Fiona, but it would be both impolite and rash for him to use it. She returned his smile, and some colour came to her face. There was no opportunity for conversation, for at that moment Halfhyde found evidence of a wind, a light one, from the north, and he called for'ard to the Captain. McRafferty waved in acknowledgement and came running aft with the First Mate, who was already shouting for the hands to stand by the braces. The wind failed them again after they had made a little progress, and once again they lay becalmed, but not for long. As though that wind had been a harbinger, a fresher blow came and kept up steadily and for long enough to clear the doldrums, to the relief of all hands. Within a couple of days the *Aysgarth Falls* had picked up the south-east trades and had begun the tack down towards the tip of the South

American continent, into the offshore area where the Pampero blew from the pampas of the Plate, with its rapid fall in temperature, its teeming rain, its thunder and lightning that played around the masts and yards and sent frightening crashes down through the ship to shake her very frames. Then, as they dropped further south and came into the westerlies roaring around Cape Horn, the winds that blew without cease right around the world in the High South Latitudes, life became an apparently endless battle against wind and sea, and the call from the poop was constantly for all hands, with every man working to fight the ship round into the South Pacific, enduring a frozen, wet hell as McRafferty tried to find the elusive shift of wind that would carry him into gentler waters. It was a grey, dreary time of no hot food, no fires to dry out clothing, frozen fingers pulling the nails out on the ropes, sea-sores, nipped flesh and gashed arms and legs. Goss, the saloon steward, was kept busy with his medical chest, putting on plasters and bandages with the assistance of Fiona McRafferty, temporarily released from purdah in the interest of sending the hands back to duty as soon as possible.

Halfhyde became one of her patients, having suffered a deep cut on his right forearm as it was caught by a stranded wire in the standing rigging. While she cleaned the wound with soap and precious water Halfhyde tried to draw her into conversation during one of Goss' absences from the saloon, asking her how many times she had made the passage of the Horn.

'Oh,' she said lightly, 'I can't remember. A lot of times. I'm quite used to it.' She hesitated, then went on, 'Father told me you had been round – once, I think he said.'

'Twice. Out and home. Outward bound aboard a battleship, the *Meridian*. It's easier in steam. You can disregard the wind.' The short exchange ended when Goss came back; the steward's cold, unresponsive manner seemed to make the girl close in on herself and become formal, as though she knew he would carry tales to her father.

At last the shift of wind came and was taken full advantage of and soon after this the *Aysgarth Falls* was round Cape Horn and into easier waters, though still tacking into the teeth of the westerlies, which called for expert handling of the canvas. Both McRafferty and Bullock showed their qualities: both were first-class seamen, as Halfhyde had been quick to recognize from the start. But now he began to recognize something else: McRafferty, though always the master when it came to the handling of his ship, gave the impression that he was playing it carefully where Bullock was concerned. Just little things; a touch of arrogance in the First Mate's manner that was inappropriate towards the Captain, arrogance that brought no rebuke although McRafferty looked put out; muttered conversations out of hearing of the hands, when McRafferty's face developed a scowl and he seemed ill-at-ease. Halfhyde had the notion that the First Mate had some kind of hold over the Captain, and once again he thought about the passenger waiting in Iquique.

* * *

Someone else had got wind of that passenger: the seaman named Float, the knife-bearer who had joined with Halfhyde back in the Mersey. Float had overheard a conversation between McRafferty and the First Mate and he broadcast it around the fo'c'sle. 'The Old Man's uneasy,' he said. 'Don't go much on the idea, 'e don't.'

'Why?' Shotgun asked without much interest.

'I dunno.'

'Who's the passenger?'

'Dunno that either.'

'Don't know much, do you,' Shotgun said witheringly. 'In any case it's not our worry. Won't affect us, we're just the scum.'

'Speak for yourself,' Float said. He didn't regard himself as scum at all; he was proud of his gaol record, proud of his conviction for grievous bodily harm in particular. It set him up above the rest, did that, showed he was a hard case. But he also knew that, hard as he was, Shotgun was harder. Shotgun had dropped hints that in America where the gun was the law, he had killed men. Nothing specific, just the casual hint, but

Shotgun looked a killer. Float, angered by the remark about scum, wanted to retaliate. His face was as sharp as that of a rat as he peered about him and fixed his attention on Halfhyde, a softer option in Float's view than Shotgun and a handy butt for his spleen. He said in a flat voice, 'Mister bloody Halfhyde's not scum. Oh, no! Mister Halfhyde's a gennelman, hoity-toity voice an' all – ain't that right, Mister bloody Halfhyde?'

'Yes,' Halfhyde answered coolly. 'I'll not deny what's true just to keep in your good books, Float.'

'You won't, eh? What's a gennelman doing in the fo'c's'le of a windjammer? Remittance man, are you, chucked out by 'is family as a bum?'

Halfhyde shrugged. 'My business is not your business, Float, but you may believe what you wish about me.'

'What about answering the question? That's polite, ain't it?' Float looked round: he had stirred up interest, the off-watch seamen were all eyes, staring through the shadows brought by the guttering oil lamp swinging in its gimbals over the table, all staring at Float and Halfhyde. Fights and blood-letting broke the monotony of life at sea. Float said again, 'That's polite. Gennelmen, they're always polite. Now, if they're rude, they knows what they gets, don't they?'

Shotgun was watching, eyes narrowed. He said, 'Put a sock in it, Float, Halfhyde's all right. He's a good seaman and that's enough for me. Better seaman by far than you, you stupid bastard.'

Float's head jerked up sharply. 'You call me a bastard?'
'Yes.'

In the fo'c's'le of a windjammer, that particular insult couldn't be, never was, ignored. Float got to his feet, his knife suddenly in his hand as if by magic. Halfhyde rose as well; his naval instincts were all for stopping fights at sea in the interest of the ship. But Shotgun beat him to it; Shotgun was on Float in an instant, leaping on to the table and diving for his man. Float crashed backwards, his knife-hand crushed flat against his chest as muscular arms went round him. Shotgun began to beat his head into the deck but Float managed to squirm clear, wriggling a wiry body free of the American. He still held the

38

knife; Halfhyde saw the lamp-light glittering from the blade as Float lunged towards Shotgun's neck. It swept in an arc, stopped suddenly as Halfhyde grabbed the arm and twisted it up behind the body. There was a yelp of pain, then Float, slippery as an eel, broke free as Halfhyde knocked over a slop bucket and almost lost his footing in the greasiness of the resulting mess. As Float lunged towards him, another man intervened. Float's knife sliced into the throat, and the man fell, gushing blood. As Float withdrew the knife and stood at bay, and lunged again towards Halfhyde, his arm made violent contact with the smoking oil lamp.

The lamp lifted, swung free of its hook and dropped with a crash, spilling oil. Within seconds the fo'c'sle deck was running with flame. A number of the hands dashed out as the place began to fill with smoke and Halfhyde was left to fight the fire with old Finney, the shanty-man, and the American, Shotgun.

FOUR

'Fire buckets!' Halfhyde shouted. 'Away you go, Shotgun.' The American ran out on deck and Halfhyde heard the desperate clatter of the water-pump as the red-painted buckets were taken down from the rack and filled. Halfhyde set Finney to the task of helping him drag out the donkey's breakfasts, the straw palliasses that formed the bedding. As he did so Bullock's voice was heard, shouting the hands back to fight the fire. The acting Second Mate, O'Connor, organized a chain of men to pass the buckets, and as soon as each one had been emptied on to the flames it was sent back to be refilled. Halfhyde and old Finney, assisted now by two of the apprentices, got the palliasses out just in time: the flames were now licking at the woodwork of the bunks, while in the centre of the messroom the heavy table was on fire and blackening.

Feeling the singe of his clothing, blinded by thick smoke, Halfhyde felt for the buckets as they were passed along. He flung them over the blazing woodwork. He could scarcely breathe; he stumbled over a couple of bodies lying on the deck. Alongside him he heard O'Connor's voice, cursing as the heat scorched his exposed flesh. As the fire began to come under control, Halfhyde left the buckets and began dragging the suffocating men clear of the fo'c'sle, sweating like a pig as he did so. Bullock was working like ten men, tirelessly. Captain McRafferty had come for'ard from the poop, his face anguished as he saw what was happening to his ship. His home and his living were in jeopardy. His relief was enormous when the First Mate reported that the blaze was dying down.

'Thank God, Mr Bullock, thank God! What was the cause of it?'

'I don't know', Bullock said harshly. 'But I'll be finding out.'

'Do that, Mr Bullock, as quickly as you can.' McRafferty wiped sweat from his face; his hands shook as he did so. 'Fire at sea . . . the worst thing that can happen to any master.' He looked aloft: he'd been lucky. Fire could spread fast, and once it got a grip on the mass of ropes, on the sails, and ran along the wooden decks and into the cargo holds, a ship would burn to the waterline before the sea doused the flames.

* * *

Float was bowled out quickly enough: Shotgun lost no time in reporting the facts to the First Mate, and Float was hauled aft to the poop, none too gently, by Bullock himself. In the meantime a number of the fo'c'sle hands plus O'Connor and the carpenter had been overcome by the smoke and when Halfhyde had dragged them clear he saw that both O'Connor and the carpenter, together with one of the seamen, were dead, in addition to the murdered man. Float was now charged officially and the facts were noted by McRafferty in the log.

'You are scum,' he said to Float. 'You put in jeopardy the lives of every soul aboard my ship, and you have killed one man and have been responsible for the deaths of three others. You will be landed into police custody the moment we berth in Sydney, or perhaps in Iquique.' McRafferty turned to the First Mate. 'Mr Bullock, you'll have the man handcuffed and placed in leg-irons and accommodated in the fore peak.'

'Aye, aye, sir,' Bullock answered. He laid hold of Float's shoulders and propelled him in a bum's rush to the poop ladder. Lifting him, he flung him bodily down to the waist. Float lay in a heap on the deck, moaning. Bullock slid down behind him and kicked him brutally to his feet, then once again sent him spinning along the deck to fetch up against the bulwarks by the foot of the mainmast.

That day there were more sea committals and afterwards Halfhyde was sent for to go to the saloon. McRafferty was seated alone at the long table; Bullock was on watch on the poop above. McRafferty said. 'I'm told you rendered good service to my ship this morning, Halfhyde.'

Halfhyde shrugged. 'My duty, sir. Nothing more, nothing less.'

'True. But you saved the ship, and many lives.'

'Did Mr Bullock report that, sir?'

McRafferty gave him a shrewd look. 'No. The fo'c'sle hands did. Also, I saw for myself.' He paused, running a roughened hand over his chin. 'You don't like Mr Bullock, I fancy.'

'Nor him me, sir.'

'I warned you he was a bully. But he's a good seaman and a hard worker.'

'I'm aware of that, sir.'

'Good.' McRafferty gave a bleak smile. 'You may wonder why I should be discussing my First Mate with a fo'c'sle hand?'

Halfhyde said shortly, 'The thought crossed my mind, sir.'

'Then I answer this: I wish you to make an effort to get along with him, for you will be working together as officers. I'm making you acting Second Mate, Mr Halfhyde, until I can find a replacement, which will not be before we reach the Australian coast – anything available in Iquique would be ullage.'

'Why not promote your senior apprentice, sir?'

McRafferty said, 'You may as well have asked why I didn't do so rather than promote the bosun in the first place. The fact is my senior apprentice is very far from experienced – which you are not, at least in regard to the sea itself and the handling of a ship.'

'And my lack of a certificate as Second Mate?'

McRafferty shrugged. 'Needs must when the devil drives, Mr Halfhyde, and I have no one else that I would trust. It is in any case a formality – you have only to apply to the Board of Trade for a certificate of service and it will be granted, as you're aware. That is one reason why I have chosen you.'

'And the other reasons, sir – apart from the unavailability of anyone better?'

McRafferty stared him in the eyes and said enigmatically, 'So that you will be closer to me when I wish to make use of your

42

services. Kindly transfer your gear from the fo'c'sle to the Second Mate's cabin, and take over the watch on deck from Mr Bullock at eight bells.'

* * *

There were black looks from the fo'c'sle hands when Halfhyde went for'ard to gather his small amount of gear together; they did not take kindly to one of their number being set above them, and a man so recently joined at that. In their view he had been promoted to the afterguard simply because he was a 'gennel-man' and spoke with a lah-de-dah voice that before long would grate like a saw on the Old Man. When Mr Halfhyde was despatched back to the fo'c'sle he could watch out.

Halfhyde went aft feeling that every man aboard, with the sole exception of the Captain and the old seaman Finney, was against him; and he knew that he would need to watch his every move. There was enmity on the poop as well when he went up to take over from the First Mate, who had been livid at his appointment. Bullock had needed to be given the facts about Halfhyde by the Captain; it was unprecedented for a mere fo'c'sle hand to be so suddenly elevated to the afterguard and Bullock's tone was sneering, following the line already taken in the fo'c'sle.

He stared Halfhyde up and down. 'Quite the gentleman. It seems it takes *that* rather than seamanship to get a Second Mate's berth these days.'

'I'm no mean seaman, Mr Bullock, as you must have learned by now.'

'Not slow to praise yourself either, it appears.'

Halfhyde said, 'I know my worth and have no intention of demeaning it.'

'Just put a foot wrong,' Bullock said, 'and I'll do the demeaning, don't you worry! The Queen's ships may be all right for those that like them, but there's more to seamanship than spit and polish and kiss my arse. Crawlers aren't welcome aboard any merchantman, *Mister* Halfhyde, as you'd do well to bear in mind.'

43

Halfhyde grinned. It was an icy grin. He said, 'Let us take your opinion of me as read, Mr Bullock. I'd be obliged if you'd now hand over the watch – in a seamanlike manner.'

For a moment it seemed as though the First Mate was about to strike him down, and Halfhyde clenched his fists in readiness for a fight. He would give as good as he got; Bullock knew this – he'd not forgotten the damaged hand he'd collected when Halfhyde had first reported aboard in Liverpool. Scowling, the First Mate handed over the watch and then, after a long look aloft at the set of the canvas, went down the ladder to the saloon. Halfhyde could hear his harsh voice coming up through the skylight as he greeted Miss McRafferty. Halfhyde turned away and began pacing the poop, hands behind his back, aware of the surly manner of the man at the wheel. That man would have overheard all that had been said, and it would go back to the fo'c'sle the moment he was relieved that the First Mate had no more time for the Second than the crew had. Nevertheless, it was pleasant enough to be once again in charge of a watch, to feel that all depended on himself, his eye and his quick judgement. Pacing, Halfhyde's mind went back to his days in the Queen's service – his active days: he was not forgetful of the fact that he was still on the half-pay list as a lieutenant and that one day he might be recalled to serve again on full pay afloat in a man-of-war, though the chances of another command might now be much less. Their Lordships of the Admiralty tended to have long memories, and if they had not, then they would quickly be reminded by senior officers of the fleet that Lieutenant Halfhyde had in his past cocked a snook or two at higher authorities.

* * *

The *Aysgarth Falls* backed her tops'ls to lie off the port of Iquique shortly after dawn on a brilliant, clear morning. McRafferty was on the poop with Bullock and Halfhyde as the flag signal for a pilot was hoisted. McRafferty was looking thoughtful and anxious; Bullock's face had a half smile on it and once again there was the strong impression that to some

44

extent McRafferty was in pawn to his First Mate. One of McRafferty's problems was, it appeared, the disposal of the man Float. McRafferty was disinclined to hand over any British subject, murderer or not, to what he called dagoes, a word that brought back to Halfhyde many memories of Captain Watkiss, Royal Navy, who had referred to all foreigners of whatever complexion as dagoes – even the Chinese had been dagoes to the strutting pomposity of Captain Watkiss. Bullock's view was that McRafferty should be guided by the advice of his agent in Iquique, a Scot by the name of Mackinnon, who would come off with the pilot and the representatives of the Chilean port authorities.

'The dagoes'll demand my log, Mr Bullock. Then it'll be out of Mackinnon's hands.'

Bullock shrugged. 'We should wait and see, sir. We must take what comes on that point. Float's scum. We have other concerns that must not be forgotten.'

'Yes, yes, you're right.' Captain McRafferty walked to the fore rail of the poop, gesturing the other two to follow him out of earshot of the helmsman. Then he addressed Halfhyde, sounding formal. 'I am taking a passenger on to Sydney, Mr Halfhyde.' He didn't want Bullock to know he had already spoken of this to Halfhyde. 'This is not being arranged through my agent. No mention of a passenger is to be made in Mr Mackinnon's hearing, do you understand?'

Halfhyde nodded. 'Yes, sir. You may depend upon my discretion.'

'And your obedience,' Bullock said before McRafferty could speak again. 'Do you understand that as well, eh?'

Halfhyde glanced at McRafferty; the Captain seemed ill-at-ease and muttered that Bullock need not concern himself about Halfhyde's obedience. Bullock disagreed. He said roughly, 'That's all very well, Captain. He must be warned, now he's been told —'

'He had to know, Mr Bullock, he had to know.'

'Well, that's as maybe and you could be right, I'll agree. But he'll have to toe the line when we make Sydney. If he doesn't, he'll have me to reckon with. I just wanted him to know that for sure. I'm not an easy man. Got that, *Mister* Halfhyde?'

Halfhyde answered coolly. 'I shall of course obey any order from the Captain, Mr Bullock.'

'And from me.' There was steel in Bullock's voice and as his hand moved inside his pea-jacket Halfhyde saw the muzzle of a small revolver staring him in the face.

* * *

The pilot and a number of officials came off with a smoke-belching steam tug and the *Aysgarth Falls*, with her sails furled, was taken inwards to the anchorage, where under Bullock's directions an anchor was let go in a cloud of reddish dust from the windlass. Mackinnon, the agent, a small sandy man with a freckled face, chatted with McRafferty on the poop and when the ship had got her cable the two men went below to the saloon accompanied by Bullock to deal with the port officials. Halfhyde was left to see to the clearing up of the decks and the overhauling of the running gear; and to deal with the bumboats that came off from the shore and clustered around the accommodation-ladder and below the bulwarks, offering wares of all kinds from fruit and articles of clothing to the services of women who for a price would be made available to the crew the moment they were permitted shore leave.

'Bloody likely,' old Finney called down. 'There won't be no shore leave, not if I knows the Old Man. 'Arf of us'd desert, or so 'e thinks, then 'e'd 'ave to 'ang around till 'e could get a new crew shanghaied aboard.' Finney spat into the water. 'Why I ever went to sea, Gawd knows.'

Halfhyde happened to be alongside him. 'You know very well why, Finney,' he said.

Finney looked round. 'Why's that, Mr 'Alf'yde, sir?'

Finney was the only man aboard to address Halfhyde respectfully; and Halfhyde knew why. A conversation whilst coming up the coast had revealed that Finney had once been captain's coxswain aboard a man-of-war. After serving nearly twenty years in the Queen's ships he'd disgraced himself by returning aboard drunk in Malta and had been disrated down to able seaman; that had been more than he could take and when his time was up he'd come ashore gladly; but had found no niche for a seaman away from the sea, so had returned to the only trade he knew, this time in the windjammers. Halfhyde answered his question. 'You went to sea because you damn well wanted to, Finney. You're a born seaman. Every hair a marline-spike, and —'

'Every drop o' blood a drop o' good Stockholm tar. Aye, sir, that's about right. But it's not much bleedin' good, sir, if the urges of the blood can't be satisfied now an' again.'

Halfhyde lifted an eyebrow. 'At your age, Finney?'

Finney spat once again over the side. 'Age ain't got nothin' to do with it,' he said in an aggrieved tone. Grinning, Halfhyde turned away and went back to the poop. Voices, raised in argument, came up from the saloon below. The law was being laid down by someone, probably, Halfhyde thought, the port authorities; and McRafferty was countering it. Soon after this the shoreside visitors left. The Chileans went over the side into their waiting boat accompanied by the agent, Mackinnon, and Bullock. McRafferty saw the party away, then called to Halfhyde.

'Mr Halfhyde, Float remains aboard. I was able to stress that the murder took place upon the high seas, not inside Chilean territorial waters. He will be handed over in Sydney.'

McRafferty went below, seeming pleased to have won his point; but Halfhyde sensed trouble ahead. A man facing hanging for murder was a nasty kind of cargo, one that brought a disagreeable spirit to the ship, a kind of portent of disaster.

Ten minutes later McRafferty's voice came up through the skylight. 'Mr Halfhyde, a word with you in the saloon.'

FIVE

In his years in the naval service, Halfhyde had seen few harbours as bleak as that of Iquique and what it must look like in foul weather was best left to the imagination. Even today it was uninviting, a nasty little port on the fringe of the Atacama Desert, with the Western Cordillera of the Andes mountains rearing distantly behind. Among other things, the town was liable to devastation by earthquake. Yet Iquique was an important place on the seafarer's map and the anchorage was crowded with shipping, both sail and steam, though sail predominated. Halfhyde had looked from the poop at the ensigns of many nations besides Britain: there were German ships, Scandinavians, American, French, Portuguese and Spanish.

He found no enthusiasm for setting foot ashore; but the shore was where he was being sent. McRafferty said, 'You told me in Liverpool that you had been to Chile before, and that you have some Spanish.'

'A little Spanish, yes. I've never been to Iquique. Only to Valparaiso and Puerto Montt. And once only.'

'No matter, you have some acquaintance with the country, Mr Halfhyde.' McRafferty pulled at his side whiskers. 'I have a mission for you, one that is not to be mentioned outside this saloon – that is, so far as the ship's crew is concerned.'

Halfhyde lifted an eyebrow. 'Mr Bullock, sir?'

'Precisely.'

'Mr Bullock is already ashore. Iquique's a small enough place by the look of it. Suppose I meet him?'

48

McRafferty answered impatiently, 'Iquique is not as small as all that. Bullock has gone with my agent to the offices of the Nitrate Combination to make arrangements in regard to my cargo. If you should happen to meet him in the port area, you shall say simply that I have allowed you shore leave so that you may see a port that is new to you.'

'And the real reason for my run ashore, sir? Is it to do with your passenger?'

McRafferty nodded. 'I wish to learn more about him, Mr Halfhyde. The only possible source of information is, I believe, a certain good friend I have in Iquique. Even he may know nothing of this man, but it's worth a try.'

'As you say, sir. And his name?'

'The name of my friend is Aguirre Trucco. The name of my passenger . . . this I do not yet know.'

'Then how —'

'Señor Trucco is a knowledgeable person, Mr Halfhyde, one who keeps an ear to the ground and an eye lifting for trouble. If, for instance, there is any person in Iquique awaiting a ship so that he can escape the law, extradition perhaps, then it's a pound to a penny Trucco will know of him. If Trucco knows nothing of any such person, then I would feel safer in bringing a passenger aboard. Do you understand?'

Halfhyde said, 'I understand, sir. But if your friend does know of such a person, how will you be sure that it is your passenger? Even if you knew the name, he could be using a pseudonym – and very probably is, if he's up against the law.'

'I realize that. But at least I shall be warned that there may be trouble.'

'You'll still take him aboard?'

McRafferty looked away and answered obliquely. 'I shall discuss the matter further with Mr Bullock.'

* * *

Crossing the anchorage in one of the importunate bumboats whose crew had been persuaded by a little silver to act as ferry, Halfhyde reflected that discussion with the First Mate would

49

be likely to result in Bullock putting two and two together and guessing that there was collusion between the acting Second Mate and the Master, at any rate if Bullock should get wind, as surely he would, of Halfhyde's visit to the shore. But that was for the future; currently Halfhyde's thoughts had flown somewhat acidly homewards to Portsmouth: mail had awaited the *Aysgarth Falls*, brought ahead of her by a steamship out of the London River, and that mail, coming aboard with the agent, had contained a letter from Sir John Willard addressed to My dear Halfhyde and ending Your father-in-law, John Willard. In between, coldness could be detected. The admiral wrote that Mildred had been fretting and, upset by Halfhyde's sudden departure across the world, was disinclined to put pen to paper herself. She believed there was a lack of love and consideration, a view apparently shared by the admiral, and also by Lady Willard who had been, very clearly, the instigator of the letter. There was an implied threat that if his absence continued beyond the normal limits of a voyage out and home, then it might be expedient for the Admiralty to be informed. If that was done, then Halfhyde would find himself out on his ear, since he had proceeded overseas without permission from their Lordships.

Halfhyde had sworn roundly and then crushed the letter in his fist. The admiral had gone on to write that Mildred proposed spending the next few weeks with cousins near Newmarket. By the letter's date, she would most probably be there now. Halfhyde wished her joy in her surroundings.

The bumboat entered the port and Halfhyde scrambled ashore on to the jetty, where a number of ships were loading or discharging cargo and the air was blue with the shouts of the foremen stevedores as the crates and sacks were trundled up and down the gangways. Picking his way over the usual seaport litter, a scene not unlike that of Liverpool, Halfhyde left the dock area and walked on into the town. At this time of the day the seamen from the ships were little in evidence; there was work to be done aboard, and the only manifestations of liberty were a number of drunks lying in the gutters or in dirty side alleys off the main thoroughfares. To Halfhyde's eye the town was similar to Valparaiso but on a smaller scale; every other doorway seemed to lead to a brothel or drinking den and the place appeared filled with pimps, greasy men who sidled up to Halfhyde and tried to interest him in their wares.

He pushed them aside, to be followed by imprecations as he stalked on. He had not far to go; Aguirre Trucco ran a ship chandlery close to the docks. Captain McRafferty had given him precise directions; he had no difficulty in finding the premises whilst keeping a weather eye open for any sign of Bullock, of which there was none.

Halfhyde entered; the place was not busy. The hour was as yet early for the bosuns and stewards, carpenters and sail-makers to come ashore to conduct their business. Halfhyde recognized the proprietor from McRafferty's description: a small, bright-eyed man behind a counter, wearing a large apron that threatened to obliterate him altogether.

Trucco beamed and kneaded his hands. 'Buena vista, señor,' he said.

'Good morning, Señor Trucco —'

'Engleesh?'

Halfhyde nodded and approached the counter. 'English, yes. I come from a friend of yours.'

'Yes?'

'Captain McRafferty of the *Aysgarth Falls*.'

'Ah, so! Yes.' Trucco smiled in a friendly fashion. 'An old friend, yes, whom I have served for many years. You come for provisions, yes?'

'No,' Halfhyde said. 'This isn't a business call of that nature and I'd be obliged, and so would Captain McRafferty, if you'd not mention my call. I'm Captain McRafferty's Second Mate and his business is private. So —'

'Si, si. Private. Then you must come into my house. One moment, please, señor.' Trucco went through a door at the end of his counter and called. A smiling, buxom woman appeared: Señora Trucco, who would take over the store. Trucco beckoned Halfhyde to follow him, and turned back through the door. Halfhyde was led to an office, barely furnished with a desk and some shelves and a couple of chairs.

51

Bidden to sit, he lost no time in stating what he had come for. Trucco listened closely, nodding at intervals. Then he said, 'I understand the anxieties. I also know – though this perhaps I should not say – that Señor Bullock has fingers in many pies, not all of them good ones. You will not repeat this.'

'I will not. But may I ask how you know this, Señor Trucco?'

Trucco shrugged. 'He has been sailing for many years to the Chilean coast – many times to Iquique, long before he joined Captain McRafferty. There has been talk that has reached me from time to time.'

'I see. And the passenger for the *Aysgarth Falls*? Do you know who he is?'

There was another shrug. 'Possibly. Possibly not.'

'Which means?'

'There are always many persons seeking passages out of Iquique. Some for good reasons, some for bad. It is very easy to board a ship illegally . . . the port authorities are lax and only too susceptible to bribes, as perhaps you know.'

Halfhyde didn't comment on that; he was disinclined to speak of his lack of merchant ship experience, to go into his antecedents and the many explanations that would have to follow. He said, 'I'll put my question differently. Have you any precise knowledge of any person who might embark aboard the *Aysgarth Falls*?'

Trucco shook his head. 'I am sorry. I have not. Only in a general way . . . I have heard that there are persons in the town who are seeking passages without too many questions . . . but as I have told you, señor, that is not unusual in Iquique or indeed in Valparaiso, or Callao, or —'

'Yes, quite. These persons – do they seek passages to England, or to Australia?'

Trucco shrugged. 'To many places, those included.'

'I see. You can say no more than that?'

The Chilean didn't answer at once. He sat for a moment in thought, his face creased up like a monkey's, then he got to his feet, went to the door, and opened it enough to take a quick look up and down the passage. Closing it, he went to the window, which he had shut on entry in spite of the increasing heat of the day, and looked out carefully. Then he sat again, drawing his chair close to Halfhyde. 'One must be very circumspect, señor. My family, my business, my own life also – all could be at risk. But for Captain McRafferty I am willing to take a risk, and your face tells me that you will not cheat. It is an honest face, a man's face – as a ship's chandler I see all sorts and can form opinions that are seldom proved wrong.' It could have been McRafferty speaking, as he had done back in Liverpool.

Modestly, Halfhyde inclined his head, hiding the smile that was forming. He said gravely, 'Thank you for your trust, Señor Trucco. I shall not betray it if you have something to tell me.'

Trucco said, 'There is a person, such as you enquire about. I cannot say if he is the very one, but I have heard that he wishes to take passage to Sydney. If this is the one, I would advise Captain McRafferty to refuse him passage.'

'His name?'

'Cantlow'

'British?'

'Yes. A sergeant of dragoons, a deserter from your British Army.'

'A strange place to find such a man, señor?'

Trucco shook his head. 'Not so. Men come to Iquique from many parts. This one is said to have deserted from his regiment at Cape Town, and to have sailed to Valparaiso by signing aboard a steamer that left the Cape after the, what do you say, huing and crying had died down —'

'And his reason for desertion? Is this known?'

'Not to me, señor. But I can put two and two together. When drunk here in Iquique, this man talked of having been in the vicinity of the Kimberley diamond mines and it is said that he showed a small bag, and that this bag contained diamonds.'

'So you're suggesting he's concerned with diamond smuggling?'

'Yes, this is likely, I think. And he is in a hurry for a passage since showing the bag.'

Halfhyde laughed. 'That I can understand! His life's in

53

danger from thieves without a doubt. Do you know where he's to be found, Señor Trucco?'

'No. His tracks he will have covered very well. But I would suggest that for you to look for him is unnecessary. You will warn Captain McRafferty, and he will refuse passage to this man. The rest of it need not concern you. You are not the law, señor.'

'True enough. But there are reasons why it would be better for me to find this man and establish whether or not he is the one due to come aboard the *Aysgarth Falls*. If he's not, then I'd not wish to deprive Captain McRafferty of a paying passenger. If he is . . . well, then, perhaps I can persuade him to look for another ship, for I believe that if he were to present himself for embarkation, Mr Bullock would see to it that he was not turned away.'

'But Captain McRafferty —'

'Would suffer in the end – yes, I know, and I would wish to preserve him intact, as would any loyal officer.' Halfhyde leaned forward. 'Señor Trucco, as a good friend of Captain McRafferty, I ask you for any further help you can give.'

* * *

The Chilean had not been able to offer much; he genuinely did not know the current whereabouts of Sergeant Cantlow. All he could do was to give Halfhyde an address in the town where he might, just might, be able to pick up further information. The information, he said, would for a certainty be there, but the acquiring of it would not only be virtually impossible but also a task of the most extreme danger: the given address was that of a clearing house for persons wanting to get out of the country by sea and no questions asked. It was well enough known through the criminal grapevine and was also, Trucco said, known to the police; but no arrest had ever been made there. For one thing it was too dangerous to police life, for another palms had been well greased. The clearing house was left severely alone and if things went wrong for him Halfhyde would find no help from the police – even if he was given time to get away before the

54

knife went into his back. When he had seen that Halfhyde was determined to find Sergeant Cantlow, Trucco had, with obvious reluctance, passed him the means whereby he might gain admittance: he was to say he came from Red Danny's. Red Danny was an Englishman who ran an exit agency in Valparaiso under cover of a boarding-house, the sort whence unwary men were shanghaied to sea aboard the outward bounders short of a crew. It would be up to Halfhyde himself to invent a story to account for his movements as far as Red Danny's together with a reason for wanting a passage. He would be entirely on his own; and he would need to move fast before a check was put on him with Red Danny in Valparaiso.

Halfhyde went deeper into Iquique, still watchful for Bullock, still pushing aside the pimps and prostitutes and the younger element, the small boys with sisters to sell as a form of early private enterprise. The sisters' charms, vividly described, fell on deaf ears as Halfhyde strode along. Pulling out his watch, he found the time to be ten-thirty-five; there was no hurry. The *Aysgarth Falls* was not due to sail for Australia until nine o'clock that evening, after being brought alongside to load her part cargo of nitrates. It was possible the passenger intended to board disguised as a stevedore – Halfhyde had been given no information on this point by McRafferty, who very likely didn't know himself. Bullock, who would presumably know, wasn't giving anything away.

Meanwhile Halfhyde was thirsty; and authenticity was all. It would do no harm to have the smell of whisky on his breath when he reached the clearing house. He entered the next drinking establishment he came to and approached the bar through thick smoke from pipes and cigars, pushing his way through a crowd of Chileans and a sprinkling of seamen, obvious as such from their clothing, nearly all of them three parts drunk. Music was being played: a guitar, and on a stage at one end of the sizeable room a woman pranced in the nude, grinning and gesticulating, doing all manner of things with an empty whisky bottle – endeavouring to pick it up with a part of her anatomy never designed for such an activity while the seamen and others roared their approval in many languages

55

and urged her on to further demonstrations of versatility. Halfhyde, who had seen such acts before in other parts of the world, turned his back; yet smiled at the wicked thought that Mildred might well have had her mind broadened if she were present. The further image of Mildred herself performing in such a manner made him give a guffaw of laughter; which appeared to annoy a big man wearing a heavy black beard and earrings in the lobes of his ears.

'What's the bloody joke, eh?'

'Only my thoughts, friend, only my thoughts and nothing to do with you.'

'Saucy,' the man said, sounding belligerent. 'That's what I bloody calls you, saucy. An' I don't like your bloody voice, so shut it.'

'Anything to oblige,' Halfhyde said mildly but with a gleam in his eye. 'If you like, I'll lick your boots. They could probably do with it.'

'Eh?'

'Never mind.'

The man was very drunk; he lurched and almost fell, then said, 'That voice. It don't fit with Iquique. Nor does your rig. Dressed like a seaman, sound like a bloody lord. What's your game, matey? On the run – are you, eh?'

'No more than you, I dare say.'

Pig-like eyes stared at him, red-shot and bleary. There was a belch. 'What you done, matey?'

'Nothing to do with you, my friend.'

'No?' A hand shot out and took him by the throat. It squeezed, but not hard, then it fell away. 'Fix you up, I can . . . if you make it worth my while. What about that, eh?'

Halfhyde put a finger to his lips. 'Not here, friend. Let's be sensible. In any case, I'm not in need of assistance from you.' Once again the hefty hand came out and laid hold of his throat, this time squeezing hard. No one took any notice; the naked woman was now attempting to pick up a silver dollar thrown on to the stage and all attention was riveted. Savagely Halfhyde lifted a knee and jabbed vigorously in a vital place. There was an oath and the squeezing figures came away, ready to ball into a fist, but Halfhyde grabbed the wrist before the man could strike. He decided to take a chance; it was a hundred pounds to a penny that the man was also on the run from the law. He said, 'No help wanted. I'm fixed up. I come from Red Danny's.'

'Red Danny's, eh.' The eyes focused a little better on Halfhyde; the mention of Red Danny's seemed to bring a touch of sobriety. 'You'll buy me a drink on that. Whisky.' The hand came down on Halfhyde's shoulder and he was pushed against the bar. The man shouted for whisky, and a bottle and two glasses were placed before them. Halfhyde's new mate had also passed through Red Danny's hands. When they'd had a skinful, he said, he would personally escort Halfhyde to the clearing house.

Although he had his directions from Trucco, Halfhyde acquiesced; partly because he now had no alternative, but also because to arrive with someone known to the establishment might give him some extra authenticity. He reckoned he could have struck lucky. But as it turned out, the luck was not due to last.

SIX

It was only a short walk. The man swayed along, not talking now. Halfhyde propped him up as the legs went in all directions. They turned off into a narrow, unpaved alley of mean dwellings; half of them appeared to be derelict but yet inhabited by poor families with many children and mangy, half-starved dogs that bared their teeth and snarled as the two men passed by. From here they turned into another alley; Halfhyde recognized his destination from Trucco's description before his drunken companion had stopped at a heavy door set into a whitewashed wall with the roof of a building visible beyond.

The man banged at the door, and they waited.

The door was quickly opened by an old woman, bent and withered, dressed in black. As she admitted them she mumbled something in Spanish, something that Halfhyde didn't catch. As the crone shut and bolted the door behind them, they made their way across a dirty, littered courtyard towards the building whose roof had been seen beyond the outer wall. Still lurching, the bearded man led the way to a door at the side, which he jerked open. It swung back; inside, a window, though dirty, gave some light. Three men were visible, sitting on an earth floor with their backs against the wall. As his eyes became accustomed to the dim light, Halfhyde saw more men to the left of the door.

Halfhyde's companion gave a hiccup. 'Brought a mate,' he said. 'Where's Espinoza?'

One of the sitters answered in English. 'Gone down to the

docks. Who've you brought, Raby?'

'He's come from Red Danny's.'

The sitter got to his feet and came close. He looked dangerous; he said, 'Your friend's supposed to say that for himself, Raby.'

'He did. Said it to me.'

'You've been drinking, Raby.'

'None o' your business if I have.'

'No? We're all dependent, one on another, so long as we're here. You know that.' There was steel in the voice, and a clear threat. The bearded man seemed subdued. The speaker turned to Halfhyde. 'I'll not ask your name, since you'd not give your true one. But I want your story and I want it now.'

'Certainly,' Halfhyde said. 'May I know who I'm talking to?'

'You heard what I just said. What applies to you, applies to me. If you want a name, let's say it's Smith. All right?'

Halfhyde nodded. He had his story ready and he gave it. He'd fallen foul of the law down south in Valparaiso: he'd been short of funds and he'd helped himself, a case of embezzlement of money belonging to his employers, a mining company. Certain contacts had led him to Red Danny's, and Red Danny had kitted him out as a seaman but that had been as far as he could assist at that time. There was a greater chance of finding a passage out of Iquique and he had been sent north. And here he was. He said, 'I was told down in Valparaiso that I'd find another British subject here. Maybe that's you.'

The man nodded. 'Maybe. What name were you given?'

'Cantlow.'

'I'm not Cantlow.'

That, Halfhyde thought, was probably true; the man had no military aspect and indeed looked more like a seaman. 'Is he here?'

'No. I'm the only Britisher. So there's no Cantlow, whether the name's true or false.' The man paused. 'You've told me your story. I don't promise you can be helped, that's not up to me. You'll have to wait for Espinoza.' There was another pause and again there was a threat in the voice when he went on, 'Espinoza may have more questions to ask.'

'Then I shall answer them,' Halfhyde retorted evenly, and sat down like the others. The man addressed as Raby had already slumped to the ground and lay in a heap, breathing stertorously. The air in the room was close, thick with humanity and the fumes of whisky coming from Raby. Halfhyde took stock of his situation. If this Espinoza was handling McRafferty's passenger, he could already have removed his human cargo to be handy for embarkation. Halfhyde looked around warily. The men had a comatose look mostly, an aspect of resigned apathy. Possibly they had had a long wait in the clearing house and they had acclimatized themselves to inactivity, preferring not to leave the place as Raby had done in case they should miss a suddenly announced sailing. They were a mixed bunch, some young, some old, some with their crimes almost written upon their faces, some with expressions of apparent innocence. Halfhyde sat in mounting impatience, knowing that he could be wasting his time. The wait in fact lasted a little over an hour, then footsteps were heard approaching the door. There was more than one man. The first in was thin-faced, dark, and was probably, Halfhyde thought, Espinoza. The next was a man like a gorilla, thick, deep-chested, heavily beared and with longish hair. But there was a swagger in the walk, and the bearing was erect, the eyes hard and challenging, and there was the unmistakable stamp of the soldier.

Behind him came Bullock.

* * *

There had been no avoiding the First Mate. The man who had questioned Halfhyde on his arrival with Raby had drawn Espinoza's attention to the newcomer. As Halfhyde got to his feet, Bullock's face was murderous.

'What's this mean? What are you doing here?'

Halfhyde smiled icily. 'That is a question I might well ask you, Mr Bullock. I think you're engaging in a very dirty trade, and acting strongly against the interests of Captain McRafferty. I shall ask you to desist, or —'

'Or nothing.' Bullock thrust his face close and brought out the revolver Halfhyde had seen aboard the *Aysgarth Falls*. 'I warned you not to cross me. Just look around you, Halfhyde. You don't imagine you're coming out of this, do you?'

Halfhyde had no need to look anywhere; all the recumbent forms had got to their feet, seeing their safety under threat. The soldierly man's eyes blazed in the light from the window, and he took a pace forward. He was pushed back by Bullock. In a thick voice Bullock said, 'Leave him to me. Just leave him to me. I've a score to settle, and he's mine.'

Halfhyde saw the fist come up, and he moved fast as he had done in Liverpool. Bullock was caught for the second time. Missing target, he was carried on by his own impetus and almost fell over. As he came back in, Halfhyde swung at him and gave him a glancing blow that almost tore off an ear. Bullock swore viciously, gave his head a shake, and lashed out blindly. He had no finesse and Halfhyde parried him neatly and easily enough. But in the long run there was no chance; as Bullock went down flat with blood pouring from his mouth after a smashing left, Halfhyde was taken from behind by the man of military bearing, a heavy blow to the head with the muzzle of a revolver, and he fell beside Bullock, out like a blown candle.

When he came to his senses, with a violent, throbbing head, he was alone and no longer in the room where he had been struck down. He was in total darkness and although he was not bound there was a feeling of constriction; reaching out and around, his hand contacted cold, damp walls set very close. He tried to sit up despite a spinning head, and that head smacked into what felt like stone. After a moment of near panic, he tried to relax and think out his situation, to force his mind to clarity. There was air; no sense of undue difficulty in breathing. Therefore there must be some contact with the world outside, though scarcely anything large enough to permit escape.

There was also total silence.

That he was in some kind of a cellar he didn't doubt, but the silence must indicate that he was not below the room where the men had been sitting out their wait for a ship. They could not all have been shipped out together. Escape from Chile was a matter for individual negotiation – it must be. Thus he was in some other part of the building or even possibly right away from it. In Iquique, the carrying of a supposed drunk through the streets would arouse no particular interest from passers-by.

Why hadn't he been killed already? Was he, in fact, to be killed at all, would release come when the *Aysgarth Falls* was safely away, if she wasn't already? He had no idea of the time; his watch was still with him and was ticking, but in the total darkness he couldn't read its face. But he hadn't been there all that long; there was no stubble on his face and the blood he felt beneath his eyes and in his hair was still sticky. He rolled over and began an exploration of the dank cellar, the cellar that was more like a stone coffin. There had to be an entry somewhere. It didn't take him long to find it: a square recess above his head, blocked by a heavy segment of stone. Not surprisingly, it was immoveable from below.

* * *

For the hundredth time Captain McRafferty looked at the brass clock on the saloon bulkhead and then went along the alleyway to the door that gave access to the waist. The ship had now been moved to the loading berth and Bullock was supervising the removal of the cover from the after hatch in preparation to take the part cargo for Sydney. McRafferty said, 'I'm anxious about Halfhyde, Mr Bullock.'

The First Mate wiped a hand across his ginger moustache. 'Likely he's jumped ship. Found the life too hard for his lily-white hands.' He paused, staring at McRafferty. 'Better not to have let him go ashore.'

'Possibly. But I doubt if he's deserted. I fear some harm may have come to him.'

Bullock grinned. 'Iquique's a funny place for the unwary, Captain, as we all know well enough.' He looked away from McRafferty, shading his eyes along the loading quay. 'A lazy place, too. There's no sign of our cargo – it should have been ready for us.'

'And the man Jesson, Mr Bullock – my passenger?'

Bullock said, 'All arrangements made. I told you, he'll come aboard after dark.' He sounded impatient. 'There'll be no trouble, not this end of the run, anyway.'

McRafferty nodded and walked away, hands behind his back. His chief worry with regard to his passenger was the Australian arrival. So far the First Mate had been unwilling to discuss this, insisting that all would be well and there was no need for any anxiety. Difficulties would be overcome but Bullock refused to commit the passenger in advance: Jesson would have made his own arrangements for his reception and they, the shippers, would have to comply with his requirements. McRafferty went aft to the saloon and found Goss pushing a duster around the mahogany furnishings.

'Whisky, Goss,' he said.

'Aye, aye, sir.' Goss brought out the bottle of Dunville's and a glass. McRafferty took a large one, thoughtfully, his hand shaking a little. He was liking the prospect of his passenger less and less, and was more and more resentful of his First Mate's manner, but now he was deeply committed and no less in need of the passage money than before; and he would be very relieved when Halfhyde returned aboard. McRafferty felt more than ever that the presence of Her Majesty's commission at his side would be a comfort.

* * *

The cargo was sent aboard in the early evening and after that the hands were put to work again, cleaning down and seeing all shipshape for the long haul across the Pacific for their Australian landfall off Sydney Heads. They turned to with many grumbles; the Old Man was a bastard, not allowing them any shore leave. They had been both sober and continent for too long, longer than it was reasonable to expect any man to be. The mutters reached the afterguard but McRafferty disregarded them; the hands must put up with it, and Bullock went for'ard to tell them so in no uncertain terms. If they didn't shut their gobs and pull their weight, there would be a few heads sore from the First Mate's fist. They worked a little harder thereafter but the grumbles continued in lower tones. As the day darkened towards dusk they were sent below, only the night watchman remaining on deck. It was Finney who took the first trick and there was a stir of interest when he went below on being relieved from his watch and reported the embarkation of a passenger.

'A toff,' he said. 'A real toff, frock coat an' all, an' fancy boots. Name o' Jesson. Came in a cab an' paid it off in gold.' Finney sucked at his teeth. 'Bleedin' mass o' gear I 'ad to hump aboard, too! Reckon the Old Man, 'e's goin' to do well on the passage money.'

Below the poop, Mr Jesson was settling into the spare cabin, attended by Goss. He spoke little, stood waiting ostentatiously for Goss to leave, and Goss took the hint. There was something about the passenger that had a scaring effect on the steward, as if at any moment Mr Jesson, like a mad dog, might bite. When he was alone in the cabin, Jesson, scarcely able to move for the amount of gear that stood around him in his heavy leather cases, reached into the capacious pocket of an ulster that he had carried aboard himself over his arm and brought out a revolver. This he put into a drawer beneath the bunk. Locking the drawer, he removed the key and slipped it into a pocket of his frock coat, glanced at his reflection in the mirror above the wash-hand basin, and stepped out into the alleyway.

He met Bullock.

Bullock asked, 'Is everything all right, then?'

He got a cold look. 'Yes. At what time do we make sail?'

Bullock pulled out his watch. 'We'll be away in a shade over an hour.'

'Good. I don't want any delay. Now I wish to speak to the Master.'

Bullock indicated the saloon. 'He's in there. With his daughter.' He saw the gleam that came into the passenger's eye. 'A word of warning. The Old Man watches that girl like a hawk. He'll crack down hard on any hanky-panky.'

'When I want your advice, Bullock, I'll ask for it,' Jesson said loudly, and turned for'ard towards the saloon. Bullock flushed, took a step towards him, then shrugged. The passenger was paying, after all, and paying very well indeed, and Bullock had a fifty per cent interest on account of his own services in the matter. There were things that had to be accepted.

* * *

It was some while before anyone came to Halfhyde; by the time the stone block was lifted clear from above, he had given up hope. He was to be left to die, his body sealed for all time in a hole in the ground that might well arouse no one's interest until he had been reduced to a heap of bones. He had drifted off into a state of semi-consciousness and when the stone was lifted away and yellow light came down from a candle-lantern held high in a man's hand, he fancied for a moment that he was seeing beyond the grave and glimpsing the other world. But the voice that came down to him was no heavenly one: it was that of his earlier interrogator, the man who had refused to give any name beyond Smith.

'Up,' the voice said, sounding hollow. 'Or are you too weakened?'

Halfhyde sat up, feeling a brief period of light-headedness. He said, 'Far from it. I'm consumed with eagerness to be out of this place if that's your intention.'

'It is. Come up.' A hand reached down and steadied Halfhyde as he thrust head and shoulders through the opened square. He was assisted through; he found he was in the open air at one side of the courtyard and that a light wind was blowing to stir up the dust; also that it was now after nightfall. A revolver had now appeared in the man's hand. Above it, in the lantern's light, the eyes were watchful. The man said, 'Careful now. I'll shoot if I have to.'

'And disturb the peace?'

There was a laugh. 'In Iquique the peace is always being disturbed. No one takes any notice of gunshots.' There was a pause. 'Your friend Bullock told us about you, Mr Halfhyde . . . a half-pay lieutenant of the British Navy, so he said. Is that right?'

'I have that honour, and you would be well advised —'

The man interrupted. 'Bullock wanted you to be killed. We told him that would be done and that nothing would come out. He paid well for our silence – for Espinoza's silence. We wondered where such money came from, so much gold. Then we were told, I shall not say who by, that Bullock's passenger was the man you'd mentioned earlier.'

'Cantlow?'

'Yes. He's known to be worth a lot of money – the little mystery was solved.'

Halfhyde said between his teeth, 'And now my ship will have sailed – with Sergeant Cantlow on board presumably, and my Captain standing into much danger because of him!' Frustration mounted; if he could make a getaway it might not be too late. If the authorities or the British consul could be informed, the *Aysgarth Falls* might be overhauled by a steamer and Cantlow taken off. At this stage McRafferty could very probably keep himself in the clear but if the affair was allowed to continue he would commit himself irrevocably by attempting, as he would have to attempt, a clandestine landing on the Australian coast. Halfhyde made a sudden movement towards the man with the gun, but was forestalled. His arms were seized from behind by a man he had not been aware of until now, and a voice in his ear told him, in Raby's now sober tones, to take it easy.

The man with the gun said, 'That's two warnings. You'll not get another. You won't be killed, but you'll be disabled.'

Halfhyde pondered this remark, then asked, 'Should I take it that you have a use for me – one, perhaps, not known to Bullock?'

'You're quick in the uptake, Lieutenant Halfhyde! The answer's yes. As I told you, friend Bullock believes you dead by now. You would have been, had he not told us your name. When he did, why, then matters took a different and more profitable turn.'

'My name?'

'Yes, Lieutenant Halfhyde. It's known in Chile – known to us as well . . . it's not so long ago —'

Halfhyde broke in. 'You spoke of a different turn. May I ask in which direction the turn leads?'

There was a laugh. 'North, to the port of Arica. You have been in Chile before, Lieutenant Halfhyde ... and you've made powerful enemies.'

SEVEN

Enemies in Chile: there was no doubt whatsoever that Half-hyde had been much in disfavour in certain quarters of the country, and in quarters more highly placed than the proprietors of the clearing house. He had upset the Chilean Government itself, and his first thought was that General Codecino, General Oyanadel, or even President Errazuriz himself, might be after his blood. All of them had suffered very red faces as the result of Halfhyde's successful intrigues in cutting out Captain Watkiss' squadron from under their noses, down south in Puerto Montt; and extracting a British traitor, by name Savory, from the clutches of their allies the Germans. But all this was in the past; Halfhyde had thought at the time that Codecino and Oyanadel might well have faced firing squads after his departure in punishment for their ineptitude, not to say their chicanery against their own country's interests. It was true, however, that no word of such had ever reached him and it was possible that the good generals had proved resilient enough to placate their President.

But it turned out that it was not the Chileans who were in the minds of his captors. His current enemy was one of longer standing, although one much concerned in the Chilean débâcle and with Savory, one whom Halfhyde had outwitted too often in the past to be forgiven. The man who called himself Smith said, 'There is a squadron of the Imperial German Navy in the port of Arica. Three first-class cruisers, under the command of a vice-admiral. I doubt if I need to tell you his name, Lieutenant Halfhyde.'

68

Halfhyde swore. 'Paulus von Merkatz,' he said softly.

* * *

The journey was an uncomfortable one, made in a closed carriage with a gun held against his ribs on either side. The carriage rocked and jolted on broken springs along the appalling road north out of Iquique. Halfhyde had plenty of time to ponder on Vice-Admiral von Merkatz, whose squadron had been despatched to Chile on that previous occasion to collect Savory and his intimate knowledge of the British plans for naval expansion. Halfhyde's stratagems as urged upon Captain Watkiss had resulted in von Merkatz' own flagship being damaged; and he had outwitted the German again in the waters of the River Plate between Uruguay and Argentina. And on an earlier occasion von Merkatz had been left fuming and impotent in the hands of the Customs and Excise in Plymouth Sound, while Halfhyde, whose misleading manoeuvres had forced him in, cocked a victorious snook from the battleship *Prince Consort* . . .

Halfhyde had asked how von Merkatz knew he was aboard a windjammer and had entered a Chilean port.

'He doesn't,' Smith said with a laugh. 'He's due for a happy surprise.'

Halfhyde lifted an eyebrow. 'I see. In that case, how did you —'

'We hear many things along the grapevine, Lieutenant Halfhyde. Now and again we handle deserters from warships – British, Spanish, Germans have passed through our hands. Since we're in this for the pickings, we listen. And we learn. And we forget nothing, since one day it may come in handy.'

'Like now.'

'Yes, like now.'

Halfhyde sat back, saying no more. From Iquique to Arica was around a hundred and twenty miles. The journey would take all of four days, perhaps longer. If he remained in these men's hands for that length of time, the *Aysgarth Falls* would be perhaps a thousand miles out to sea if the wind stood fair for her. Although her track was known, it was never an easy task to intercept a ship at sea, the more so when she was under sail and at mercy of the wind's vagaries. And if he reached Arica and was delivered into German hands, then he could assuredly say goodbye to the *Aysgarth Falls* and Captain McRafferty and indeed to his own plans for the future. Von Merkatz would have him placed in cells and would sail with him for the Fatherland, a prize to be presented to his Emperor who would then take his revenge for damage caused over the years to his ships and his pride. The British Admiralty might well be indisposed to recommend action to Her Majesty on account of a half-pay lieutenant who had already incurred their displeasure; and Vice-Admiral Sir John Willard in Portsmouth might be only too pleased to be rid of him as a son-in-law.

It was a devilish prospect. It must not be allowed to happen; but to get away would be easier said than done. The man who called himself Smith was vigilant, so was his companion sitting on Halfhyde's other side. The captive was worth money; no doubt there would be bargaining with von Merkatz and Halfhyde had no doubt that the German would be generous. Halfhyde made the assumption that he would be hidden away somewhere in the port, while an emissary went aboard the German flagship, or more likely, so as not to be held as a kind of hostage against Halfhyde's delivery, sent a message by one of the bumboats.

Time would tell.

* * *

McRafferty paced the poop, a prey to mounting fears. Bullock had been threateningly insistent that he should make sail without more delay; the passenger, Bullock said, was restive and there would be difficulty over the passage money if they didn't clear away from Iquique fast. It was only too possible that Halfhyde had fallen victim to some attack ashore and never would rejoin. All McRafferty had been able to do was to leave word with the police authority to have Halfhyde looked for, a message that was received politely enough but with scarcely any interest. This done, the orders had been passed and the *Aysgarth Falls* had stood out to sea with the steam tug's assistance until she was outside the port with a light wind on her starboard quarter. Short once again of a Second Mate and with no replacement possible now from the villainous crowd in the fo'c'sle, the Master had been obliged to take watch-and-watch on deck with his First Mate.

As McRafferty kept an eye lifting on the set of his sails, Jesson came on deck from the saloon. McRafferty looked at him with a distaste that he took pains to disguise. Jesson looked an evil man but he had to be put up with. Already half the passage money had been paid over, and the First Mate's bargaining had been good: one hundred pounds in gold was in the Captain's safe, a similar amount was stowed in Bullock's cabin. A total of four hundred sovereigns to reach Australia from Chile was, by any standard, very good payment indeed . . .

'Good morning, Mr Jesson.'

Jesson responded with a curt nod; he was at best a monosyllabic man, McRafferty had found, and bad-tempered. Looking around at the slightly ruffled water, then down the ship's side as though to make some assessment of her speed, he said, 'We're not moving very fast.'

McRafferty shrugged. 'The wind dictates, Mr Jesson, the wind dictates.'

'Wrong. I do.'

McRafferty stared back at him, feeling the anger rise. 'Not to the wind.'

The face mottled behind the thick thatch of beard. 'I'm a wealthy man, by God!'

'Then you're a lucky one also, Mr Jesson, but no money can buy the wind.' McRafferty turned his back on a nonsensical, arrogant statement, and strode aft to the wheel, from where he cast a critical eye aloft. He could maybe get an extra knot out of her. He spoke to the helmsman. 'A shade closer to the wind, Finney, just a shade.'

'Aye, aye, sir.' Old Finney moved the spokes, bringing the wheel up a fraction. McRafferty watched for a while longer, then walked back to the rail and stood beside his passenger.

He said, 'I shall do my best, Mr Jesson, but as I told you last night, I do not expect my landfall in Australia to be in less than thirty-two days – and that assumes fair winds, fair winds all the way. Shipmasters are seldom as lucky as that. But there's no sense in fretting.'

'Thirty-two damned days aboard a ship!'

'It must be put up with, Mr Jesson.'

There was a snort from Jesson, and he turned away abruptly and went below. McRafferty gave him a moment, then moved towards the saloon skylight and stood listening. Jesson's voice was loud; he was speaking to the girl, but to McRafferty's satisfaction appeared to be getting no encouragement and after a while he stopped talking and McRafferty heard him shouting for the steward. Whisky had been part of the contract, and Jesson seemed addicted.

* * *

On the road north, there were stops at wayside hostelries, sleazy places where rough meals and a shakedown bed were provided. Halfhyde slept in a small room along with his two armed companions, who took turns to remain awake throughout each night. Early starts were made and as each dawn came up they were already on the road. There was no chance of escape; the men were much too wary. Halfhyde didn't doubt for a moment that the guns would be used if they thought it necessary, and in the privacy of the bedrooms, and in the carriage itself, his hands had been tied behind his back. Although the circumstances were different, there were similarities with Halfhyde's journey north by carriage with the Chilean General Codecino, from Puerto Montt to Valparaiso. Travelling beneath the distant shadow of the mountains, the scenery appeared much the same. But their surroundings grew bleaker as they drew nearer to their destination. Arica, according to Smith, was a lesser port even than Iquique, a mere village by comparison with Valparaiso, a place where guano, salt, copper and sulphur were exported and cargoes were landed for transit to Bolivia.

'Not', Halfhyde observed, 'a likely spot to find Admiral von Merkatz and a heavy squadron, I should have thought.'

Smith was in agreement. 'Nevertheless, he's there and is expected to remain for some while before sailing south for the Horn and the passage back to Kiel. He's said to have gone in for provisions and bunkers, after a long haul across from Chinese waters.'

As at last the carriage jolted its way into Arica, Halfhyde saw the great, grey ships of the German squadron, with the flag of Vice-Admiral von Merkatz flying at the masthead of a first-class cruiser which he recognized as the *Mannheim*. A boat was coming inshore – a steam picquet-boat, smartly manned. As he came between the hovels of the little township, Halfhyde lost sight of the picquet-boat but soon afterwards the carriage came into the port area and the boat could be seen alongside a small jetty. An officer of captain's rank, probably the Flag Captain, was walking away from it with a lieutenant and the boat's crew was evidently awaiting their return. The carriage moved on and once again the Germans were lost to sight. Before his view of the dock area had gone, Halfhyde had been able to see the other shipping lying off the port. There were three steamships and some half-dozen square-riggers. The square-riggers were Finns and Norwegians; of the steamers, two wore the Red Ensign, a fact worth noting. Halfhyde was unable to make out the flag of the third. Some minutes after this the carriage stopped at one of the hovels and Smith got down, leaving Halfhyde in the care of the other armed man and the driver, who remained watchfully upon his box.

Smith banged at the door of the hovel. The door was opened by a man who looked like a South American Indian; Smith, who seemed to be known to this man, went inside. A few minutes later Halfhyde was brought out of the carriage and hustled into the building with a gun pressing against his spine. Just as he went in there was a sudden shift in the weather: the afternoon, which had been fine, darkened with extraordinary rapidity as a large cloud swept across the sun. At the same time a wind came up, a curiously hot wind from the west.

* * *

The same wind, blowing in across the Pacific, had passed to the north of the track taken by the *Aysgarth Falls*; but Bullock, on watch as the glass began to drop alarmingly, had observed the disturbance in the northern sky and had called the Master.

McRafferty turned out at once and climbed to the poop. 'What do you make of it, Mr Bullock?'

'The nearest I can get's a typhoon, sir. You can see the perimeter of it clearly.'

McRafferty examined the sky. 'It's no typhoon, Mister. We're much too far westwards for that.'

'Typhoons can go off track.'

'Maybe, but never so far as this. You know as well as I do, they originate in south-east Asia and head north for the Philippines and the Japanese islands. We're not in the area where it would be called a hurricane, either.'

'It's a cyclonic storm of some sort,' Bullock said in a surly tone.

McRafferty nodded. 'I'll settle for that, Mister! God alone can say what's the cause of it here. In any case, I believe we shall stand clear of it – it's moving eastwards, I fancy.'

Bullock wiped a hand across his face. There was a touch of rain and a big cloud, almost black and very threatening, was extending towards them although the main route was, as McRafferty had said, easterly. 'Best get the canvas off her,' Bullock said.

'Yes, I agree. Rouse out all hands, Mr Bullock. Another hand to assist Finney at the wheel. Bring her down to lower tops'ls.' McRafferty stared towards the north, through fast-worsening visibility: the rain was sheeting down now and a moment later the heavy rumble of thunder came, apparently from right overhead as vivid streaks of lightning struck down to play around the masts and yards. McRafferty noticed an odd warmth in the wind; like the breath of hell, he thought fancifully. As the watch below tumbled out from the fo'c'sle and hurried to take their places for getting the canvas off or attending to the battening-down of hatches and doorways,

74

Jesson came up from the saloon wearing a scowl.

'Below if you please, Mr Jesson,' McRafferty shouted peremptorily.

'If there's to be delay —'

'It will have to be accepted. Go below. I'll not have lubbers cluttering my decks in a storm, Mr Jesson.'

'Now look here, Captain —'

'It was an order. At sea you will obey the Master.' Captain McRafferty moved close, thrust his jaw forward. The face when angry was a formidable one; it was Jesson who turned away, muttering angrily, a red light coming into his eyes and the lips thinning behind the beard. With an ill grace he went below, and probably only just in time to save his skin. As his head disappeared below the hatch, the *Aysgarth Falls* lurched heavily to a sea that swept below her counter and lifted her, canting the deck sharply. McRafferty reached in time for the weather mizzen shrouds and hung on for his life. Men went skidding on their backsides along the waist; and from the saloon McRafferty heard a heavy bump followed by violent imprecations. He smiled to himself, grimly. Jesson would know better next time. Soon after this there was a rising sound of fury from the wind, a shrieking, dismal and threatening whine as invisible fingers plucked at the ropes and wires. Little by little the sails were furled along the yards as the desperately working men fought to keep themselves from pitching down from the footropes. It was easy enough to miss a footing, or to over-balance when laying out across the great flapping sails to beat the wind from them and secure the canvas in the buntlines.

* * *

In Arica Smith had left the hovel; Halfhyde supposed he had made his way to the docks to contact the seamen manning the picquet-boat from the flagship and have a message passed to their Admiral. But Smith was nobody's fool. When he returned he was accompanied by two policemen, swarthy men carrying rifles and side-arms. Halfhyde was given to understand he was being arrested and moved to the town's gaol, where he would be under police guard.

He bowed ironically towards Smith. 'I congratulate you on your perspicacity,' he said. 'You were unwilling, I take it, to place your head in von Merkatz' noose?'

Smith grinned. 'I wouldn't trust him too far, Lieutenant Halfhyde. But he'll get nowhere with the Chilean authorities and he won't dare to double-cross them.'

Halfhyde made a contemptuous sound. 'Von Merkatz would double-cross his own mother, my dear fellow! His own Emperor, too, if he could be sure of getting away with it. As to the Chilean authorities staving him off, I have my doubts as to that as well. When last I was in Chile, von Merkatz stood favourably with President Errazuriz.'

'Who is no longer in office.'

'Nevertheless, Germany and Chile are friendly, and von Merkatz may see his way clear to obtaining my person without you as an intermediary to be paid.' Halfhyde knew that there could be extra danger to himself insofar as the Chilean authorities would also want his person; but the danger would most likely not be great. It was a pound to a penny that Smith had entered into a private arrangement with the local police and his, Halfhyde's, presence in Arica would never be reported to Santiago. However, he once again advanced a proposal that he had first made whilst en route from Iquique. 'Why not accept English gold, or the promise of it, instead?'

Smith didn't bother to reply; Halfhyde would never be able to muster the sum expected from von Merkatz, let alone exceed it. Halfhyde was taken from the hovel to be marched to police headquarters. The day had darkened further by this time and as the small procession came into the open the rain started teeming down. Halfhyde and the policemen were drenched within seconds. Halfhyde was ordered to double; he ran ahead between his escort, his feet splashing through mud and filth. The rain was cold but there was a curious residue of warmth still in the wind and this suggested to Halfhyde the likelihood of an approaching earthquake, not uncommon in Chile. More than ever, he wished he was at sea. The movement of storm water could at times be frightening, but the movement of solid earth was a nightmare, and would be the more so if one was locked into a police cell.

On arrival at police headquarters there was a complete absence of any formalities, which confirmed to Halfhyde more clearly than words that his arrest would not be reported beyond the perimeter of the port. Also, Smith had seemed unconcerned that his prisoner might inform the local police about the set-up in Iquique; Halfhyde for his part did not propose to waste his breath on the subject. The network of bribery throughout the coastal areas was much too strong to be breached. Halfhyde was put into a cell little more than four feet square, with just room enough for a plank bed on which he could lie doubled up or sit and contemplate the strong, metal-bound door that was locked and bolted on him. A small window, set high, gave some light; but by now the day had turned virtually into night and, standing on the plank bed to look through, Halfhyde could see nothing but the terrible downpour that was turning the ground outside into a pock-marked muddy pool.

For want of anything better to do he was still looking from the window as full dark came down. He saw the approach of a storm lantern, held high over the heads of uniformed German naval officers tightly wrapped in boat cloaks, splashing through the water.

Some while after this he was brought from the cell.

* * *

Vice-Admiral Paulus von Merkatz had changed little since their last encounter. The arrogance of eyes, face and bearing was there still, the sense of his own importance was as obvious as ever it had been in past years. So was his enmity, his personal hatred of Halfhyde. Now he was cock-a-hoop and ready to commit his Emperor to the promise of almost any sum that might be asked for Halfhyde's delivery into his hands.

'So, Lieutenant Halfhyde,' he said, sitting in the police chief's chair with his Flag Lieutenant in attendance. 'You are no longer in your Queen's service —'

'I am on the half-pay list, sir. As such I am still a naval officer, and answerable to Her Majesty.'

Von Merkatz smiled. 'Let us not split hairs. You are now Second Mate aboard a sailing ship – and you are in Arica, and your ship is not. I am told that your ship is the *Aysgarth Falls*, now bound for Sydney. I am sorry to deprive your Captain of one of his officers, but you are coming with me to Germany, and without delay.' He glanced up at his Flag Lieutenant, who gave a tight bow and went to the door where he gave an order. On the heels of it a German naval guard entered, four men with rifles and fixed bayonets under a petty officer. At another word from the Flag Lieutenant two of the seamen stepped forward and laid hold of Halfhyde, while the other two fell in behind. Von Merkatz waved a hand towards the door. 'Take him away,' he said.

Smith took a step forward; so did the police chief. 'One moment, señor,' the latter said. 'I —'

'Yes. You are concerned for your payment. The sum has been agreed – you have my promise of payment, which will be delivered to you through the good offices of our Embassy in Santiago. I have insufficient gold with me to pay you now —'

'But on board your flagship, señor —'

'Which is not here in this room,' von Merkatz said rudely, 'but out in the port, and I do not wish to delay. You have seen the weather for yourself, and you know the signs. You must take it or leave it, and whichever you do, be sure I shall take Lieutenant Halfhyde.' He had risen to his feet by this time and was moving for the door, back straight, head high, looking disdainfully down his nose at the Chileans.

Smith said, 'Just a minute. That's not good enough —'

'It is good enough because I say it is. If you dispute further, I shall take you as well, even if only to feed later to the sharks in the Pacific.' Von Merkatz looked at the chief of police, who was almost in tears and was distractedly twisting his hands in front of his body. 'You, policeman. If there is any attempt to hinder me and my seamen, the town will suffer. I have many guns. On my order, they will open and shatter your stinking little port into small fragments. And now good day to you all, gentlemen.'

Von Merkatz stalked out, followed by the Flag Lieutenant with Halfhyde in the hands of the escort. As he was marched out, Halfhyde turned and grinned at Smith. Smith was looking murderous, strongly doubting that he would ever see his reward. In spite of his situation, the man's furious face was pleasing to Halfhyde, something to remember during the days ahead. Smith was not going to find the police chief so friendly henceforward, either, and he might well find himself in bad odour down south in Iquique despite past bribes.

Outside, the rain had not abated. Not just yet; but, with the same suddenness that it had started, it stopped just as the party was marching behind the Admiral along the jetty where the flagship's steam picquet-boat was secured. When it stopped, there was an intense, eerie silence; then the wind was felt again, warm, moist, and there was a vivid crackle of lightning that arrowed down towards the flagship at anchor offshore. Her compass platform, her fighting tops and her guns stood for a moment clearly visible; when the lightning had gone, the darkness was intense. There was a rumble that might have been thunder, but was almost certainly not: following upon the close lightning, Halfhyde would have expected a very sharp crack or a full-bodied crash of rolling sound.

So would von Merkatz. He snapped at his Flag Lieutenant. 'Hurry! I think the earthquake is upon us.' He moved ahead at the double, lifting his sword scabbard clear of the ground. The party doubled up behind him and had almost reached the picquet-boat when the jetty began to shake and tremble beneath their feet. The section that contained the bollards to which the picquet-boat was made fast cracked away and lurched downwards, taking the boat sideways so that she took on an alarming list inwards. There were shouts from the midshipman in command, and the seamen ran to cut the mooring ropes. As von Merkatz reached the edge of the cracked section and began shouting furiously, the picquet-boat drifted clear and regained her trim in the water. Smoke came from her brass bell-mouthed funnel and under helm she turned away, stern to the jetty, and circled outwards.

Von Merkatz waved a fist and shouted, almost screamed

into the heavy rumbling sound that came apparently from the bowels of the earth. 'Come back in at once, you young blackguard, or by God I'll have you in irons the moment you and I are aboard my flagship!'

As von Merkatz watched for the picquet-boat to come in again, there was another heave and the jetty started to break up along its whole length. Halfhyde gave an involuntary shiver: twice in the last twenty years the port of Iquique had been razed to the ground. The same could happen here in Arica.

EIGHT

With the others, Halfhyde was cast into the water. Like the wind it felt warm, as though something beneath was heating it as a kettle would be heated. Flinging water from his eyes, he looked around. Von Merkatz was being grappled aboard his picquet-boat, a sorry sight, and the Flag Lieutenant was close behind him. As soon as the two were aboard, the boat stood off from what was left of the jetty. Von Merkatz glared about him, looking, obviously, for Halfhyde, who kept his head low. The German cruisers were in some trouble; two of them, including the flagship, were well down by the head, clearly visible in more lightning that flickered around their decks and tops. Halfhyde guessed that some shift in the sea bottom had nipped the anchors and drawn the cables down. Not far from where he trod water, the merchant ships were now adrift from the jetty, their mooring ropes parted and hanging judas down their sides. There was total confusion everywhere, and a complete absence of any Chileans; no doubt they were busy saving their own lives and property.

There was no sign of the German naval ratings who had formed the escort; not until two bodies drifted close to Halfhyde and he recognized the petty officer and one of the seamen, both with their chests stove in. There was a curious smell on the wind now, a sulphurous stench that caught at the breath. Halfhyde went down deep as, in another lightning flash, he saw von Merkatz' eyes looking in his direction. The Admiral shouted an order: he had seen his quarry. Beneath the surface, Halfhyde swam as fast as he could and as far as he could before

81

coming again to the surface; when he broke through he found himself about to bump the side of one of the steamers, a paddler, and thrust away with his legs just in time to save his life: there was a rush of water following upon a sound of engines; dollops of sea descended upon Halfhyde and he realized that he was uncomfortably close to one of the steamer's paddle boxes. There was a man on top of the box and Halfhyde raised a shout.

'Up top, there! Cast a line and bring me aboard. And hurry!'

* * *

The ship was the paddle steamer *Tacoma* of the Pacific Steam Navigation Company; she was ship rigged on her three masts, steam being used as an auxiliary to her sails. A tall thin funnel rose blackly and with an alien look through her rigging. Halfhyde was taken at once to the Captain.

'Who the devil are you?' the Captain asked. 'Were you thrown from one of the other ships, or what?'

'No,' Halfhyde said, wringing water from his clothing. 'I am a lieutenant of Her Majesty's Navy, and was about to be shanghaied aboard the German flagship. I doubt if I can convince you quickly, Captain, but I ask you to take my word for what I've said and deny all knowledge of me if the Huns should board you.'

The Captain laughed. 'I doubt if they'll do that! They'll be away to sea as soon as they can make it – like me!'

'You're leaving now?'

'I am. You'll have to come with me, I'm afraid – all the way to Australia.'

Halfhyde said, 'I find that suitable enough, Captain. When there's the time, you'll have my story – and my request for your continuing assistance.'

The Captain gave him a searching look, then said quietly, 'We shall see what it is you ask. In the meantime, you'd better go below and get a change of clothing, and a hot drink inside you, well laced. I'll send down for my steward.' He turned away; but before he could pass any orders there was a shout

82

from his Chief Officer.

'Captain, sir . . . German boat making alongside starboard.'

The Captain and Halfhyde looked to starboard; the picquet-boat was coming up. Von Merkatz, his uniform awry and filthy with the port scum, was waving a megaphone. They heard his shout, half snatched away by the wind.

'*Tacoma* ahoy. I am Vice-Admiral von Merkatz of the Imperial German Navy. You are harbouring a criminal. I demand to come aboard you!'

The Captain glanced at Halfhyde. 'I know nothing about you. Have I your word that the German's uttering lies?'

'You have, sir.'

There was a nod. 'You have the ring of sincerity at all events. I'll back you – I detest Huns in any case. What do you suggest?'

Halfhyde grinned. 'Since you ask, I suggest hoses.'

'A man after my own heart, I see!' The Captain leaned over the fore guardrail of his bridge. 'Mr Mortimer, the fire hoses. Turn them on the German.'

'Aye, aye, sir!'

Halfhyde said formally, 'A request, sir.'

'Well?'

'I have two special attributes: an ability to aim a hose straight, and a particularly strong personal dislike of Admiral von Merkatz.'

The Captain clapped Halfhyde on the shoulder. 'Then go to it!'

Halfhyde, delaying his change of clothing for the time being, went fast down the ladder to the main deck and took up one of the hoses as they were connected and turned on. His aim was as good as his word to the Captain: a stream of water took von Merkatz in the chest, bowling him over. Sounds of fury came back; and in the continuing play of the lightning Halfhyde saw the picquet-boat swing away under full helm and head towards the flagship.

* * *

Von Merkatz would not be so easily disposed of; and Halfhyde said as much to Captain Graves once the *Tacoma* was clear of the port and headed on her course for Australia.

'A tenacious man, and one who detests being bested. In addition to which, I assume he has a roving commission – his squadron will be the German Special Service Squadron, which customarily roves the world upon its Emperor's business and as often as not upon that of its Admiral —'

'I'm aware of the fact of the squadron's mission, Halfhyde.' Graves paused and stuffed tobacco into his pipe. 'I happen to be a senior lieutenant of the reserve —'

'A lieutenant RNR?' Halfhyde knew he had had a stroke of luck: the Royal Naval Reserve, formed in 1862, was composed of officers and men of the merchant service who did an annual training period with the Fleet and had contracted to be called up in time of war to serve the Queen. Graves could be a valuable ally; and Halfhyde expressed such a hope.

Graves nodded. 'I shall help you, never fear.' He added, 'You're not entirely unknown to me as it happens. I was last with the Fleet a year ago, serving aboard the *Royal Sovereign*, and your name was mentioned. You have something of a reputation, as I gathered.'

'Largely for being a nuisance to my seniors, which explains my presence on the half-pay list. But that's in the past, sir. I'm more concerned now to rejoin my Captain in the *Aysgarth Falls*, and with avoiding Admiral von Merkatz and his confounded guns!'

Graves cocked an eye at him. 'You believe he'll follow. He hasn't done so yet – but no doubt there's time. He'll be extricating his squadron from the effects of the earthquake, I imagine. Is he likely – surely he isn't – to use his guns?'

'He's very likely to in my opinion.'

'And cause an international incident?'

Halfhyde shrugged. 'He's a law unto himself, sir.'

'And doesn't stop to think?'

'Exactly. His passions take charge.'

'That's certainly the impression he gave me – outlined by the lightning, acting like a cat that's inadvertently sat on a gas lamp.'

'It happens to admirals, sir. Sometimes I suspect they can't help it. They are fawned upon too much by sycophants hoping one day to occupy their positions.'

'Possibly. But those guns. I'm not keen to put my ship and crew at the mercy of gunfire. I have my owners to consider, you know!'

'Yes, indeed,' Halfhyde agreed readily. 'But a means must be found to inhibit the use of his guns, and I've no doubt a stratagem will present itself when needed.'

Captain Graves pulled at his pipe and blew a cloud of smoke. 'A stratagem, eh?'

'I'm seldom short of them, sir. They have a habit of coming to me, though if you asked me at this moment to outline a plan, I would have to confess I've not a thought in my head.' Halfhyde had other matters on his mind as the *Tacoma* proceeded south-westerly, making little more than ten knots. He was something like four days behind the *Aysgarth Falls* already, to say nothing of his having taken his departure more than a hundred miles north of Iquique. But the vessel should not be hard to overtake, if he was on the right track. Graves was fairly hopeful that he could pick up McRafferty's ship; he doubted if the *Aysgarth Falls* was likely to keep up a ten-knot average speed and, as a sailing ship man himself until recently, and one well versed in the trade between Chile and Australia, he knew the sailing-ship routes like the back of his hand. McRafferty, he said, would pick up the south-east trades fairly quickly and would tack down towards the westerlies in the High South Latitudes and then ultimately the Roaring Forties for Sydney. It would be a slow passage for a sailing ship buffeting into head winds for most of the way; and steam would have the advantage.

'And this passenger,' he said. 'This Sergeant Cantlow.'

'Yes, sir?'

'I don't like deserters, renegades. And diamond smuggling's usually a dirty business. I don't know anything about Cantlow; but most diamond smugglers have committed murder some-where along the way, and my assumption would be that this one has a rope waiting for him somewhere. McRafferty was a

85

fool to take him aboard – but then I know the financial pressures on the old windjammers. It's a way of life going before our eyes, Halfhyde, and the ending of a race of men.'

Soon after this Halfhyde excused himself from the Captain's cabin and went out on deck. Although the ship's masts were crossed with their yards, there was no canvas aloft; Graves was using his engines and there was a rhythmic thump from below and a belch of dirty black smoke from the funnel, visible as a blacker smudge against the night's heavy darkness. The wind of the ship's passage blew this smoke aft along the deck, and down around the men on watch. Halfhyde was used to steam in the Queen's ships but had never grown to like the choking, gritty result of burning Welsh coal. He moved out on to the port side paddle box, looked down at the churn of water as the great wheel smacked its blades into it. A spray rose around him; he stared aft towards the Chilean coast, now vanished from sight in the darkness and the filthy weather. There was not a sign of a light. Neither was there any sign of a pursuit by the German squadron. The *Tacoma* was labouring badly, rolling heavily, and every now and again one or other of the paddle-wheels lifted clear to the roll, and the blades raced. Bad for the engine; and Halfhyde wondered Graves didn't save his engine and his coal while there was plenty of wind and send his canvas aloft instead. Even as he thought this he saw the Captain come out of his cabin and climb the ladder to the bridge and a moment later the Chief Officer was passing the word for the watch below to turn out.

'All hands . . . all hands on deck . . . make sail!'

* * *

By now the *Aysgarth Falls* had passed through the fringe of the storm. The wind had gone, leaving light airs behind, changeable breezes that had to be snatched at by expert handling of the braces. Jesson stood by the mizzen shrouds on the port side of the poop, his big head sunk in his chest, looking down at the work along the decks in the aftermath of the bad weather. Bullock was chasing the hands without mercy; the First Mate

86

had the notion that the cargo had shifted in the fore hold and he was down in the tween-deck investigating. When the hold had been checked Bullock came aft to the poop for a word with McRafferty; and reported that the fore peak had flooded.

'It's been pumped out now but it can flood again. There's the question of Float.' During the night the prisoner had been released from the fore peak to back up the short-handed crew, and had been kept on deck to work with the hands as the ship was cleared up and the storm damage made good. 'What do we do with him?'

'We can't put him back in the fore peak, Mr Bullock.'

'Sail locker, then?'

'Yes – if he gives any trouble. He'll have to be watched. But he's needed on deck so long as he behaves himself.'

Bullock looked aggrieved. 'I said it last night, and I'll say it again, Captain. We're no more short-handed than we were immediately after the fire —'

'We're short of Mr Halfhyde now. With so many losses earlier, every man's needed. Float remains handy to work the ship, Mr Bullock, and is to be confined to the sail locker only when not needed. That's an order.'

'It's risky,' Bullock said sourly. 'He'll —'

'The risk must be accepted, Mister. When we pick up the trades, we'll be tacking constantly and every man'll be needed at the braces.' McRafferty turned away.

* * *

Float had been accepted back by the fo'c'sle without too much bad feeling from most of the hands. Old Finney had withdrawn himself, so had Shotgun; although Shotgun had killed in the past without compunction his victims had not been his own mates. There was, or should be in his view, a camaraderie among the world's unfortunates. Most of the hands didn't think that way at all and were concerned only to keep on friendly terms with a dangerous man as they worked about the ship, and were glad enough that he was being made to do his share on deck instead of loafing all day in the sail locker and letting others do it for him. For his part, Float was busily scheming how to cheat the hangman. There might be ways for a man who had his wits about him and kept his eyes and ears open; and Float had a trick or two up his sleeve and he had something else as well: a knife. Not his own – that had been removed when he was searched earlier. He had found another in the sail locker, one that had been overlooked when he'd been put in there from the fore peak. It was long, sharp as a razor, and Float took good care no one would find it before he had a need of it. Action would have to be taken before the *Aysgarth Falls* picked up the pilot off Sydney Heads. Float had been thinking for many days past what that action could be. Further killing was not a part of Float's reckoning. He could scarcely make a clean sweep of every soul aboard, and anything short of that would be useless. There had to be another way, and he would find it; and his thoughts had already begun to revolve around the mysterious passenger, Jesson.

In the meantime he worked with a will and obeyed orders, steering as clear of Mr Bullock as was possible.

NINE

Still some way behind the *Aysgarth Falls*, the *Tacoma* was making good some record days' runs under full sail. Captain Graves had found a favourable wind that carried him nicely down into the south-east trades, a better wind than luck had given McRafferty. Three days after leaving Arica, skysails were observed ahead – a square-rigger still hull down on the horizon to the west. Graves sent down for Halfhyde and indicated the ship.

'It could be the *Aysgarth Falls*, perhaps,' he said.

Halfhyde took the offered telescope. 'We must hope so, sir.' The hope did not last long; it soon became apparent that the ship was on an opposite course: they were closing fast. As the other vessel came down upon them, Graves had the helm brought up to close her as near as the wind would permit. The ship was identified as the full-rigged *Pass of Killiecrankie* out of Melbourne for Callao. Graves took up a megaphone as they came close abeam and called across, asking if the Master had by chance met the *Aysgarth Falls*.

'Aye,' the shout came back. 'We spoke her two days ago. I have her position in the log if you want it, Captain.'

'I'd appreciate it,' Graves shouted.

There was a wave of acknowledgement followed by a pause. Then the position was called across and the ships drew apart again. With Halfhyde, Graves went to his chart-room, took up a pencil and a parallel ruler and transferred the given position to the chart, marking it with a neat cross.

'It gives us something to go on,' he said. 'We're overtaking her, that's certain at least.'

'And a good chance of finding her?'

Graves shrugged. 'I'll try to work out McRafferty's likely track from there, but it'll be by guess and by God, Halfhyde. I can't forecast the winds he'll be getting.'

'Surely if he's into the trades —'

'There's a degree of steadiness, yes. Oh, there's hope, but I'll not go further than that just yet.' They went back to the bridge. Halfhyde was in a near fever of impatience by this time but his frustration had to be contained. Graves was doing his best and the *Tacoma* was being efficiently driven: Mortimer, the Chief Officer, knew his job and the hands were a willing bunch, working for a first-class company and anxious to keep their berths. Halfhyde had no doubt that they could overhaul the *Aysgarth Falls* but knew that to do so on the right track was a proposition full of chance. That same morning all chance began to look bleak indeed. A man stationed as lookout in the foretopmast crosstrees reported smudges of smoke coming up from astern.

'Plural,' Graves said. He glanced at Halfhyde. 'Merchant ships don't travel in company. I don't like the sound of it. I believe it could be your German adversary.'

Halfhyde nodded. 'Clearly von Merkatz'll have the legs of us, sir. It remains to be seen by how much – I fancy not a lot. His cruisers are old and slow by modern standards.'

Graves said, 'Perhaps. But if it's him, it'll not be long before he has us within range of his guns, and —'

'He'll not open fire without a parley of sorts. We're in no immediate danger in my opinion. I understand your concern for your ship and crew, of course. Our best defence is to make all the speed we can, and keep ahead, so as to frustrate von Merkatz' desires for speech. I'll go aloft and see for myself, and in the meantime I suggest you use your engines. They may give us an extra knot or two that could make the difference.'

Graves agreed, and sent down for his engineer. Halfhyde made his way to the foretopmast crosstrees, where he levelled his telescope astern. After a while he was able to identify the fighting-tops of warships: von Merkatz' squadron without a doubt.

He returned to the bridge and reported. Graves asked, 'Suppose he makes a signal ordering us to heave to?'

Halfhyde gave a tight grin. 'Can you read flags, or the Morse code on a lamp?'

'Morse, no. Flags used in the International Code – yes, of course.'

'Then emulate the great Lord Nelson, sir, as I shall do, and turn a blind eye. In any case, the reading of a signal lamp was something I never managed to master aboard the Queen's ships.' Halfhyde paused, pulling thoughtfully at his long jaw, a light of excitement in his eyes at the thought of another sea-clash with Vice-Admiral Paulus von Merkatz. 'It's possible, if ignored for long enough after he has overtaken us, he'll put a shot across our bows, and that will be difficult not to see or hear.'

'Exactly!'

'But we'll not despair,' Halfhyde said cheerfully. 'I spoke of a stratagem, did I not, sir?'

Graves said sardonically, 'You did. Has it, by any chance, arrived?'

'Indeed it has, just at this very moment, precisely when needed! Have you a Blue Ensign aboard?'

Graves shook his head. 'I'm RNR myself, as you know, but have not the required percentage of reservists in my crew to be entitled —'

'Yes, I see. Then we shall go one further, sir, with your permission. I'd be grateful if you'd have your sailmaker construct a *White* Ensign by cannibalizing such other flags as he'll need for the job.'

Although looking surprised, Graves passed the order without comment or question: Halfhyde's manner had changed. It was as though he were in command himself, and Graves felt a little out of his depth in the possible confrontation of a German cruiser squadron from the bridge of a peaceful merchantman. Once again Halfhyde levelled his telescope astern. The smoke was now beginning to be visible from bridge level, and that was evidence that the ships were closing, however slowly. He turned to the Master. 'How long before we have steam, sir?' he asked.

Graves shrugged. 'As soon as my engineer can make it. He tells me his furnaces can't be hurried. The shortcomings of steam . . . but I know he'll be doing his best.' Graves' tone was sardonic; he was no more a lover of the black gang than was any other master mariner. But miracles were being achieved below; soon thick smoke began to emerge from the funnel, wreathing up through the rigging and the sails, and all along the decks the seamen began ostentatiously to cough their lungs up. No one liked the engines.

* * *

Sergeant Cantlow alias Jesson appreciated his sundowner, and more than that; the going down of the sun in the west to bring splendid colours to the sky and the Pacific, to glint red and gold through the network of rigging and bring fire to the yards, was Jesson's signal to begin the evening's drinking. He took it slow to start with, savouring the fine taste of McRafferty's Dunville's. McRafferty, leaving the watch to the First Mate, was in his cabin engaged upon some paperwork and the writing up of the fair log from the deck log. Fiona was sitting at the saloon table doing some petit point needlework.

Jesson said, 'What's that you're making, then, Miss McRafferty?'

She looked up, flushing a little. 'A sampler, Mr Jesson.'

'For your young man?'

'No,' she said. 'For my father.'

'The only man in your life?'

Her blush deepened but she didn't answer. Jesson said loudly, 'I said, the only man in your life. Is that right?'

'Yes,' she said defensively.

'A trifle dull.'

'I do not find it so.'

'Hah!' Jesson reached for the bottle and poured another whisky, splashing in just a touch of water. He sat with the glass cupped in his hands, brooding at the girl. She was an attractive

92

filly if rather too virginal for his taste, which ran more to barmaids of a forthcoming nature and well endowed as to the breasts and buttocks. Jesson sprawled back on the leather settee and reflected upon women he had known and bedded in his time at home and overseas. A sergeant of dragoons, which he must take much care not to appear to have been, was a sought-after person around the military camps and barracks spread throughout the world in the Queen's name. A swash-buckling person was any sergent of dragoons, and as Sergeant Cantlow he had outshone them all when wearing his uniform of the Sixth Dragoon Guards. With his black-plumed brass helmet, he had been a fine figure of a man, a fine fellow, and still was. The sap still rose in him; the whisky tended to make it rise more. He had found women easily in South Africa, he had found them in Chile too; but Chile was many days behind him now while Australia was yet a very long time ahead. The man Bullock had warned him, it was true; and he had seen for himself that Captain McRafferty was not to be trifled with and kept a very close eye on the filly. Caution was needed but a time would come. He could bide that time a little longer; meanwhile there was pleasure in anticipation and in imagination. Seeing himself back once again as Sergeant Cantlow of the Sixth Dragoon Guards, Jesson saw other things as well: creamy breasts bared of the massive constriction affected by young women, eager limbs, parted thighs . . . Fiona McRafferty would need awakening but Sergeant Cantlow was the man for that.

He poured another whisky, then sat staring openly at the girl at the table. She grew uneasy; and after a while gathered up her sewing and her skirts and fled for her cabin. The passenger watched with a grin as she went. Give her a little longer to get accustomed to having him around and she would soften, no longer run like a gazelle from his masculinity. All women were the same, looked scared, pretended they didn't want it, played hard to get – women of her sort, that was. There were plenty who didn't, plenty easier, but they weren't here.

Best forget Sergeant Cantlow: to grow into a new identity you had to forget the old one or you'd be sure to give yourself away one day. Jesson drank, sighed, stretched out on the settee, listening to the creak of woodwork around him and the banging and rattling of the blocks from up above as the *Aysgarth Falls* drove on through the Pacific.

On the poop, Bullock walked aft to look down at the wake and read the patent log that gave the speed and the day's distance run. While he read this off, with his back turned, Float, finishing a job of work on the ratlines of the mizzen shrouds before being locked back into the sail locker, glanced down the open saloon skylight and saw the recumbent figure on the settee. Talk originating from Goss, the saloon steward, had told Float that the passenger liked his whisky and never left the saloon of an evening before the bottle was empty. At this moment it was no more than half empty and already Jesson had a comatose look.

* * *

The German cruisers had been positively recognized shortly after noon as the fighting-tops had advanced over the horizon, growing very slowly larger until the compass platforms and then the decks and guns were seen. Over them flaunted the German Naval ensigns, together with the flag of Vice-Admiral von Merkatz at the flagship's main truck.

'A brave sight,' Halfhyde said sardonically. 'All to apprehend one half-pay lieutenant!'

Captain Graves spoke on the voice-pipe to the engine-room. The engineer responded nobly enough and the paddles whirled furiously; but they could not give quite enough speed to keep the *Tacoma* ahead and Halfhyde knew that the German squadron must be upon them by the time the sun went down and long before that would be in a position to open fire upon a helpless target if von Merkatz was insane enough to attack the British flag. The White Ensign had not yet been run up; Halfhyde preferred to keep it in reserve and trust that the sudden hoisting would deflect von Merkatz, though in fact there was no knowing how far his temper would lead him.

As the afternoon wore on, the cruisers closed the gap. Von

94

Merkatz began signalling. Graves was the first to spot the flashing lamp.

'You've not seen it,' Halfhyde said, 'and neither have I.' He turned his back and paced the bridge with Graves. Conversation languished; Halfhyde's thoughts were grim enough, not conducive to talk. Germany and its gaols loomed. Von Merkatz was a powerful man, known to have the ear of his Emperor, who was a man after his own heart, proud, boastful, convinced of German superiority in all things. Aboard his flagship von Merkatz too was thinking of his Emperor; part British, His Imperial Majesty Kaiser Wilhelm II was always disdainful of his distaff side – of his grandmother Queen Victoria, his childhood's nagger when his family had visited Balmoral and had been forced to pay heed to the autocratic old woman and listen to the appalling heathen noise from the bagpipes of her Scottish guard. The mere thought of his grandmother always sent His Imperial Majesty into a temper. England and the English he detested and it was frequently his pleasure to imitate and poke fun at his Uncle Edward, Prince of Wales, portly and often drunk, an easy-going fool who was said to hobnob with tradespeople such as Thomas Lipton aboard his yacht. Lipton and Dewar, tea and whisky, so common . . . von Merkatz paced his admiral's bridge, grinding his teeth. What an appalling country, where no one, not even the heir to the throne, knew his place any more. So different from Germany, as the wretched Halfhyde was going to find out the moment the Special Service Squadron reached the great base at Kiel. Von Merkatz was not unexpectant of a personal welcome by his Kaiser upon his return from foreign waters. Kaiser Wilhelm would be most pleased with his catch; His Imperial Majesty was well aware of what Lieutenant Halfhyde had done in the past – how could he not be? – and had indeed been frigid towards von Merkatz for having allowed it to happen, though von Merkatz had managed to talk his way out of that.

Now the tables were about to be turned.

Von Merkatz looked through his telescope, then spoke to his Flag Captain. 'The dolt evidently has no intention of answering my signals. Well, we shall see! Man and arm your guns, Flag

Captain, and make a signal to the rest of my squadron indicating what I am doing.'

'Yes, sir.' The Flag Captain hesitated, then asked, 'Are they to man and arm as well, sir?'

Von Merkatz stared crushingly. 'Against a puny merchantman, half sail, half steam, like one of these new-fangled motor carriages married to a windmill? Poof!'

He turned away and strode the holystoned planking of the admiral's bridge, his neat beard quivering with anticipation.

* * *

Rumours concerning the passenger had flown like bees about the *Aysgarth Falls*. Largely, these had started as a result of old Finney's report of his apparent wealth: all that heavy gear, the clothing, the assured manner. Float, who was well enough acquainted with the manoeuvrings and intrigues of the criminal fraternity, had come to the conclusion that Jesson was up to no good. The rumours had been diverse: Jesson, who was automatically assumed to be travelling under an alias, was a duke bound on some secret mission for the Queen and for the requirements of diplomacy had to travel incognito. He was one of the Prince of Wales' valets, going to Australia ahead of His Royal Highness to see to the procuration of women for the royal dalliance whilst away from his mother's court. He was a millionaire escaping from a tiresome wife and about to elope, on reaching Australia, with a younger woman. There was also those who, like Float, said Jesson was on the run after some crime that had paid off very well indeed.

For his own purposes, Float was going to find out more. Tonight was as good an opportunity as any; more so, since the man detailed by Bullock to put him in the sail locker was Althwaite, the seaman who had joined the ship with him and Halfhyde back in Liverpool. Althwaite was an unscrupulous man and not squeamish. As they approached the sail locker, Float had a word with Althwaite.

'That Jesson.'

'Yer?'

96

'Rich, we all know that. I want to take a look in 'is cabin. 'E's three parts drunk, in the saloon. There'll be pickings, what you can share in. Likely, you an' I, we'll be rich too.'

Althwaite scratched his head, his lower jaw hanging forward. 'What you asking?'

Float winked. 'Bit o' carelessness. You don't secure the hatch proper. No one'll know – promise, cross me 'eart. They won't know 'cos, give me an hour from now, you'll come back and do the job proper like. By then I'll be back inside. All right?'

Althwaite's jaw sagged lower. 'What about bloody Goss?'

'Leave Goss to me,' Float said. 'You on?'

'Well . . . yer.' Althwaite hesitated; something seemed to have penetrated. 'Look, what you want with pickings, eh? You're for the 'igh jump. You won't want no pickings, mate.'

Float said, 'Leave that to me an' all. Now – just don't bloody lock me in.'

He went inside and pulled the hatch shut. Althwaite fiddled about outside, then Float heard footsteps going aft along the waist. He went to the hatch and pushed carefully; it opened. Float thought, so far, so good. He was under no illusions that Althwaite wouldn't try to nab all the pickings for himself, lock, stock and barrel, but he could deal with that too. He waited a little in the sail locker's darkness then brought the knife from its hiding place and opened up the hatch and slid out on deck like a shadow in the night, keeping close to the break of the poop, where the sail locker was situated and where he knew he was invisible from the poop itself.

TEN

The crash and thunder of a single gun echoed across the darkening water and a splash appeared on the port side of the *Tacoma*, just off the bow. The German flagship had come up on their starboard side and had reduced speed a shade so as to hold her station.

'That's it, then,' Halfhyde said. 'Run up the White Ensign, sir, if you please.'

Graves nodded at a seaman standing by on the bridge. The man went off at the double and within three minutes the red St George's cross with the Union flag in miniature was flying from the gaff. Halfhyde said, 'Now we must hope that'll put the cat among the pigeons of the Fatherland. I believe it will.'

They waited; there was no more gunfire. Instead, the German flagship altered a little to port and came closer to the *Tacoma's* starboard beam. A voice bawled at them through a megaphone. 'Lieutenant Halfhyde!'

Halfhyde grinned and also took up a megaphone. 'Here, sir, present and correct!'

'What does this mean, the White Ensign of your confounded Navy?'

'The meaning is simple,' Halfhyde called back. 'The *Tacoma* is now one of Her Majesty's ships. As a commissioned officer of the Queen, I have exercised my prerogative to press her into the naval service —'

'There is no such prerogative!'

'I say there is, and that your knowledge of the British Fleet is inadequate.'

98

'Such nonsense! So typically English! Your Admiralty will give no backing to such rubbish, Lieutenant Halfhyde.'

'On the contrary, sir. They are always quick to appreciate initiative, and are equally quick to deprecate offensive action against Her Majesty's ships. You will be adjudged guilty before the world, sir, of – of piracy and even of *lèse-majesté* and —'

'Do not be impertinent, Lieutenant Halfhyde! Your wretched Queen Victoria, she is nothing to me, to the Fatherland, and I am inferior to no one other than my Emperor. I *command* you to take down the White Ensign!'

Halfhyde spoke aside to Graves. 'This fish has taken the hook to some extent, sir.' He brought up the megaphone again. 'Your commands are but words and will be disregarded. The White Ensign remains. If you open fire upon one of Her Majesty's ships again, you will stand condemned in your Emperor's eyes as well as those of all the world. I doubt if the Fatherland wishes to go to war, sir.'

He lowered his megaphone. To Graves he said, 'I think that's enough for now, sir.' He was about to say something further when there was another shout from the German flagship.

'If I were to sink you, Lieutenant Halfhyde, who is there to know?'

Halfhyde answered, 'Your ship's company, sir, who would be sure to talk in time. And even they would not condone wholesale murder of British seamen, just for your personal revenge and satisfaction.'

* * *

Still shadow-like, Float slid past the door of the steward's cabin, which was shut. Unseen, he entered the passenger's cabin; the door of it stood open and there was no one there. Softly he closed the door behind him and looked around in the light of a hanging lantern already lit by Goss against Jesson's tumbling in due course, half drunken, into his bunk. Working in silence, Float tried the drawers beneath the bunk; all were unlocked save one. The unlocked drawers contained nothing beyond clothing. Float cursed beneath his breath and turned his attention to the leather cases that littered the small cabin. In point of fact, they had a more interesting look than the drawers. He moved towards them, eyes narrowed. Jesson's booty, stolen goods?

Float selected the smallest of the cases – not so small as all that, in fact, but heavy for its size. He pulled the knife and a length of wire from inside his seaman's jacket. The picking of locks came easily to him; the case stood open and Float thrust a hand in.

He felt a number of wash-leather bags of varying sizes, tied around their throats.

He brought one out, excitement rising like a fever. His fingers trembled as he pulled the cord free and opened the neck. He held the bag beneath the lantern and looked at the contents.

Diamonds!

Lovely, beautiful diamonds. The bag was filled with them. Float's throat went dry. He brought out more of the bags. All diamonds; and the case contained a score or more of such bags. Very likely the other leather cases also contained diamonds. It was a king's ransom, a hundred kings' ransoms.

Float's lips formed a whistle but he managed to hold on to it. He had never expected to find wealth on this scale; and for the possessor of it to seek passage aboard the *Aysgarth Falls* when he could have booked a comfortable voyage in a steamer – or even bought his own steam yacht and done it in real style – positively confirmed to Float that Jesson was on the run with his loot.

For a moment Float sat back, considering his own situation. The light from the lantern flickered from the diamonds. The temptation to delve in and take a handful or two was immensely strong; it had to be resisted. Certainly Jesson was unlikely to realize he had been burgled until he was away from the ship, perhaps not even then; and even if he did, then no suspicions of theft would come Float's way if his friend Althwaite performed as promised and came along to lock him back into the sail locker. But Float wouldn't have any use for a cache of diamonds once the ship reached the Australian coast and he was handed over to the peelers. The whole object of his current expedition had been, in fact, to find some way of not being handed over and he had to remember that and stick fast to it. He had found what he believed he would find: evidence that Jesson had something to hide. And what a something! Jesson would want to preserve that; in Float's good time his knowledge of Jesson's haul would be made use of to ensure that he got out with the passenger, that he wasn't around when the *Aysgarth Falls* berthed in Sydney. Of course, he had no idea what Jesson's plans might be in regard to final disembarkation, but he would find out and then work things his way.

He restored the bags, re-tied, to the case, which he closed with a small snap. Gently he opened the door and looked along the alleyway.

All clear.

He emerged. Snores came from the saloon: that would be Jesson. Float padded along towards the door giving on to the open deck below the break of the poop. From that door it was just a step to the sail locker. Float waited inside the alleyway until he heard footsteps on the poop – McRafferty, who had the watch while Bullock slept. When the footsteps made aft, then Float would come out into the deck shadows.

He was all set when Goss came out of his cabin.

* * *

When the next dawn was up the German warships were still in company. They steamed in Line Ahead behind their Admiral, who was maintaining his station off the starboard beam of the *Tacoma*. Halfhyde examined the Admiral's bridge through a telescope: there was no sign now of von Merkatz. Halfhyde paced the bridge; he had persuaded Captain Graves to go below to snatch some sleep, and the Chief Officer was on watch. Halfhyde pondered his next move, and the likely next move of the German. Von Merkatz would be beside himself with fury; it would not be in character for him to withdraw, but he was going to look a very foolish man if he remained in company all the way to Sydney, only to be refused entry through the Heads by the Australian authorities – which would surely be the case. Foreign navies were not expected to enter British or colonial ports other than by prior arrangement at diplomatic level.

So what would he do?

Not for the first time in his seagoing career Halfhyde wished there was means of communication between ships at sea and the Admiralty at home – or between a ship such as the *Tacoma* and other ships that might be somewhere in the vicinity. If only he could make contact with a British squadron, such as the Detached Cruiser Squadron which might or might not be in the Pacific, then he could have met any threat from von Merkatz with superior gun power. On the other hand, the Admiralty might well wish to steer clear of trouble and would do no more than shilly-shally . . .

Would von Merkatz try to board? If he put an armed party aboard the *Tacoma* to seize Halfhyde, he would be in violation of sovereign territory but at least he would not have caused damage and loss of life. It would be a much easier situation for him to talk his way out of afterwards. But to board a ship steaming as fast as his own ships would be so difficult as to be virtually impossible. Yet would it? The German had a knot or two in hand, and, given time, could draw ahead and then let a boat drop back upon his quarry with orders to grapple and send armed men swarming up behind the grappling-irons. For a certainty Nelson would have tried it.

Meanwhile there was a kind of stalemate. Halfhyde listened to the German bugles sounding throughout the squadron as the hands were called to fall in for the start of the day's work. Soon after, the decks of the great wall-sided cruisers came alive with men, and the hoses and squeegees came out as the upper decks were washed down by barefoot seamen with their trousers rolled up to the knee. Hands were waved towards the British ships, and yells and catcalls came across, and much laughter. To the ships' companies, if not to their Admiral, the affair was a joke. They could afford to laugh; Halfhyde lifted a fist in the air and shook it back at the flagship as he noted a stir on the Admiral's bridge, much saluting, bowing and fawning as Vice-Admiral von Merkatz came up from his sea cabin.

The *Tacoma* was examined by a number of telescopes and while this was in progress Captain Graves came back to the bridge.

'Good morning, Halfhyde. He's still there, I see.'

Halfhyde nodded. 'And planning something I don't doubt.'

'But what?'

'Time will tell the way his mind is running, sir.' Halfhyde put forward his theory that von Merkatz might send away a boarding party.

Graves said, 'We shall cut the grappling-irons loose if he tries that.'

'I see dangers if we do, sir. Germans could be drowned.'

'As a result of the Admiral's order only.'

'True enough, but it could be an excuse for him – in his own eyes at any rate – to open fire.'

Graves snorted. 'Are we permitted no defence at all, Halfhyde?'

'Well, as to that, *I'm* prepared to take the risk, but I have a very particular vested interest, as you know! I shall not put your ship and crew in jeopardy, sir. If von Merkatz comes for me, then go I must. I'll rely on you to make Sydney with all despatch, and make your report to the authorities and ask for its immediate forwarding to London.'

'Of course, of course,' Graves said impatiently, 'but it's not going to come to that. There's not a man aboard who'd give in to the damn Germans and never mind the risk.'

'But I insist I shall not —'

'A moment, Mr Halfhyde,' Graves interrupted crisply. 'Mr Mortimer, I'm going below again. I shall not be long, but if there is any change in the Germans' disposition I'm to be called immediately.'

Disregarding Halfhyde, he went down the bridge ladder. Halfhyde, frowning, watched the German flagship. Very slowly now, she was drawing ahead; and soon there was a considerable signal traffic between her and the other two ships, both by flag hoist and by lamp. Unable to read the German flag code, Halfhyde could glean nothing from it but suggested to Mortimer that the Master should be informed.

Graves was quickly back on the bridge and as he came up Halfhyde saw that he had shifted into his Royal Naval Reserve uniform and was grinning like the proverbial Cheshire cat. As he came up to Halfhyde he patted the gold lace of his rank, the lace that included the straight half stripe between the two thicker intertwined ones in indication of his status as a senior lieutenant. Halfhyde, grinning back, took the hint.

'You out-rank me, sir, but this is highly unconstitutional, I fancy!'

Graves said, 'Hoist with your own petard, Mr Halfhyde. Your White Ensign was also unconstitutional, but since it's there we may as well make the fullest use of it.' He lifted his telescope towards the flagship, then added, 'Just as you have, as it were, commissioned my ship, I for my part have decided to call myself up for war service!'

* * *

McRafferty's face was like granite; but beneath it he was a very worried man. His passenger was a Jonah if ever there was one. The first report of trouble had come from that passenger when Goss had failed to appear with his early morning cup of tea; Jesson had stormed up from the saloon hatch with a sour face and a complaining voice. The pallor behind the heavy beard had been evidence, if such were needed, of the previous night's drinking. McRafferty had ordered Goss to be looked for; Jesson had reported his cabin and the pantry empty. But Goss could not be found anywhere in the ship. To make matters worse, traces of blood had been found in the saloon alleyway, close to the for'ard door on the starboard side. Then Jesson had come back to report that he believed his belongings to have been disturbed; the cases were not quite as he had left them.

'Is anything missing?' McRafferty demanded.

'Not so far as I've been able to check – no. But that someone's been at them I've no doubt at all.'

'Probably Goss, quite innocently. Cabins have to be cleaned, Mr Jesson, and Goss —'

'Well, that we'll never know now, will we? Where's Goss?

Tell me that!' Jesson waved a hand over the side. 'That's where Goss went, if you ask me, Captain McRafferty. Thrown overboard, dead! It wasn't Goss who searched my cabin. For my money, Goss disturbed whoever did, and suffered for it with his life. And you know as well as I do who did it. That damned murderer of yours, Captain.' Jesson's face had lost its pallor now; it was suffused with angry blood.

McRafferty snapped, 'You are talking balderdash, Mr Jesson, since the man Float has been securely held in the sail locker all through the night. A murderer he may be, but he's not responsible for what happened —'

'How sure are you?' Jesson demanded.

'Very sure. But to satisfy you, I shall check.' McRafferty did; an examination of the sail locker entry showed it to be securely locked; the First Mate confirmed that a man had been detailed to put the prisoner back in confinement the night before. When sent for, Althwaite confirmed that he had indeed done so. The hatch, he said, was one hundred per cent secure. When Float was brought out under guard, he looked as innocent as a baby; he hadn't even heard anything. He'd been dead tired and had just slept. He was astonished to hear what had happened. Regretting even more the absence of Halfhyde, Captain McRafferty instituted an enquiry and got nowhere. No one aboard the ship knew anything and to McRafferty their statements had the ring of truth. The only man who could have told him anything was Goss himself. Jesson once again made his point about the lunacy of Float being allowed his freedom; he made it loudly, insistently and rudely. McRafferty, all his obstinacy coming to the surface now, would have none of it. Every fit man, he said, was needed to work the ship and Float would continue to be available. With all the hands on deck, he wouldn't be able to commit murder, McRafferty said frigidly, nor would he be able to steal from the cabins. And Jesson could make the best of it and take his own steps to protect his possessions.

* * *

'What the devil is he up to now?' Graves asked in wonder. Halfhyde shrugged; von Merkatz was still drawing ahead, slowly but surely, and seemed to be manoeuvring to come across the *Tacoma's* bows. Of the other two ships, the *Stuttgart*, next in the line, had altered a little to port and was coming up dead astern of the British ship. The *Potsdam* was also coming across to port of her original course and as Halfhyde watched she came across the *Tacoma's* stern and then altered again to starboard to steam parallel with the clear intent of moving up on the *Tacoma's* port beam.

Suddenly it dawned on Halfhyde; he said, 'I don't think he means to board while he has way upon him. He's trying to get us into a corner. To box us in!'

'Force us to heave to?'

'Exactly, sir. When he's got all his ships into position, and dangerously close, he'll reduce speed. We'll be forced to follow suit. Then, when we're stopped and surrounded, he'll be able to board much more easily and with less risk to his seamen.'

'Then we'll have to stop him,' Graves said stoutly.

'We shall be impossibly outnumbered. You'll have to hand me over.'

'I shall not do that, Mr Halfhyde.'

Halfhyde gave a faint smile. 'It's a noble gesture and I'm grateful. But I shall not put you to the risk.' He paced the deck, fists beating now at his forehead. 'There must be a way. There always is. My kingdom, if I had one, for a stratagem!'

But nothing would come. The German ships moved inexorably into their ordered positions. Graves handled his ship well; but every move he made to avoid the in-closing movement was at once countered by the Germans. His ship had not the speed in hand to make a dash away to port or starboard, while the Germans had just enough in reserve to use it to the best advantage, and as the *Tacoma* paid off to one side or the other, a cruiser was always there to turn her back again. Graves had taken all his canvas off so as to make for greater manoeuvrability and so as not to be forced to obey the wind; but it made no difference to his ability or lack of it to elude von Merkatz.

Halfhyde watched the cruisers narrowly. Von Merkatz was

taking a big risk, to his own ships as well as to the *Tacoma*. The fellow must be consumed with his hatred, his wish for revenge, and was pushing matters to the limit and beyond. That could, with luck, redound to the British advantage, if he, Halfhyde, could make it so. Possibly he could; he frowned in deep thought then smacked a fist into his palm, stopped his pacing and turned to Graves.

'A favour, sir.'

'Well?'

'May I handle the ship myself, sir?'

'Do you doubt my ability, Mr Halfhyde?'

Halfhyde answered sincerely. 'By no means, sir. You know your ship better than I. But I would feel more confident *of myself* if I were to have the handling . . . like the man who tries to drive the coach when not upon the box himself, it is harder to give directions than to have the reins in one's own hands. I don't know if you follow?'

'I think I do. What are your intentions?'

Halfhyde said, 'I see a situation developing somewhat similar to a situation I've been faced with before. I believe I can handle it.' He paused, then asked again, 'Have I your permission, sir?'

Graves nodded, and stepped away from the binnacle. Halfhyde looked around, bent to the azimuth circle and took quick bearings of all three ships. Then he passed an order to the helmsman, taking the ship a little to starboard. It was an almost imperceptible movement but he knew it would show up in their wake. A few minutes later he altered a little more to starboard. On his port beam, the *Potsdam* began to follow, moving herself to starboard. As she did so, Halfhyde rang down to the engineroom for reduced speed. Soon the *Stuttgart* on his starboard bow slowed in order to hold her position *vis-à-vis* the British ship. Halfhyde repeated his manoeuvre; the German slowed still more, and as she did so Halfhyde increased speed to full and ordered his wheel ten degrees to port, thus swinging his bow fairly sharply over to starboard. From the *Stuttgart* it would have looked as though he was attempting a break-out by cutting across the cruiser's bow. The reaction was fast: the *Stuttgart* swung inwards and the water boiled up below her counter as her Captain put his engines astern to take avoiding action. At the same time the *Potsdam*, altering to keep close to the *Tacoma's* beam, came across from the British port side, just as Halfhyde swung his wheel again and passed the order to the engine room to go astern. The *Tacoma* began to slide out backwards, leaving the slowing *Stuttgart* exposed.

Halfhyde gave a shout of laughter. He said, 'Now there's a very nice inevitability about what's going to happen! The Germans, as always, have minds like slugs.'

Inevitable it was: the cruisers were now too close for avoiding action to be taken in time. The *Stuttgart* was in the position of a sitting duck, her port side all ready to take the heavy ram of the *Potsdam*. There was a shattering crash and both ships heeled violently as the ram smashed into the *Stuttgart's* bow plating. Almost at once, the latter ship went down by the head, forcing down the bow of the *Potsdam* as well. The confusion was total; a lamp began flashing furiously from the flagship, and aboard the *Stuttgart* and the *Potsdam* the air was blue with frantic shouts from the officers and petty officers. Hands ran in all directions and as the *Tacoma*, clear now of danger, put her engines ahead, the collision mats were seen to be being dragged out and manhandled for'ard with all speed.

Graves, grinning with relief, said, 'Well done indeed, Mr Halfhyde – but what now?'

'On course for Sydney, sir – or the *Aysgarth Falls* as I hope.'

'But von Merkatz —'

'Oh, he'll not follow – not yet at all events. He must stand by his ships in distress. Not even he would face his Emperor with less! You'll see, sir. But that's not to say he won't try to pick us up again later. I suggest all possible speed short of rattling the paddles off her!'

Graves was in full agreement. With joy in his heart, Halfhyde waved what he hoped would be a long farewell to von Merkatz who, as forecast, did not attempt to follow. Within the next hour the German ships were out of sight, vanished beneath the eastern horizon. The seas ahead were clear; and now all attention could be turned to the finding of the *Aysgarth Falls*.

ELEVEN

With Captain Graves, Halfhyde examined the chart, poring over it thoughtfully. By this time they were, by Graves' reckoning from the noon sight, a little over a thousand miles out from Arica. That left nearly eight thousand miles to cover to Sydney Heads.

'It's a lot of ocean,' Graves said. 'Too much to hope for a sight of any individual ship. It'd be the sheerest chance if we picked her up.' He was less confident now.

'Yet some intelligent guesses might do the trick.'

Graves laughed and straightened from the chart-room table. 'It would need an intelligence bordering on genius, Halfhyde! The vagaries of wind and sea, of individual masters even . . . no two masters think alike, you know, and no two masters take precisely identical tracks. Nevertheless, we'll do our best. I don't like to see fellow captains made into tools for evil-minded men, and this passenger of yours sounds criminal enough.' He paused. 'Deserter, you said.'

'Yes, sir.'

'And diamonds. Well, now, I wonder.' Graves bent to the chart again, then pushed it aside and took another from the drawer beneath the table, the chart for the ocean approaches to the Australian coast. Frowning, he perused it for some minutes without saying anything further. Halfhyde waited. Graves ran a pencil along the New South Wales coast, and further until the tip was running up towards Queensland and the mouth of the Brisbane River, and on again, not far short of the numberless coral formations of the Great Barrier Reef. Then down again to the Brisbane River.

He said, 'We can take it for granted, I think, that McRafferty won't be taking this man into Port Jackson – that's to say Sydney harbour.'

'A Sydney arrival is Captain McRafferty's intention, sir.'

'Perhaps, but it won't be the passenger's. Too many nosey authorities, police, customs, immigration. I think you'll find McRafferty will be overruled. I believe you said his First Mate —'

'Is inclined to take charge – yes. Also that it was he who arranged the passage —'

'Hand in glove, then, with Cantlow?'

Halfhyde nodded. 'I believe so, indeed I know that to be the case.'

'Then the passenger will not be put ashore in Sydney and McRafferty will find he has to make the best of it. The First Mate will have the whip hand. From the sound of it McRafferty is already too deeply in his grasp.'

Halfhyde nodded. What Graves had said was probably true enough; by nature McRafferty was a hard and determined man, but already Halfhyde had noted those signs that Bullock had a hold over him. Moreover, McRafferty, whether or not any deviation interfered with his cargo schedule, would be bound to take what action was open to him to keep Cantlow well clear of the Australian port authorities for his own preservation; but before McRafferty was able to appreciate that, Bullock would need to reveal the truth about Sergeant Cantlow – and once that had been done, McRafferty would be one hundred per cent committed. Halfhyde asked, 'Where, then, will Cantlow be landed, Captain?'

'Ah! That's what we have to ponder.'

'So that we'll be better able to assess McRafferty's course?'

'Well, yes, to some extent. But chiefly for another purpose, Halfhyde.' Graves tapped the chart. 'I think it would be better if we could decide where a landing is most likely – and then be there ahead of the *Aysgarth Falls*.'

'But we could be wildly out,' Halfhyde objected. 'Then it would be too late.'

'True. But I happen to know the Australian coast well, very well. Before I joined PSNC, I sailed in the windjammers . . . Iredale and Porter, out of Liverpool for South America and Australia, with many voyages along the coast between Adelaide and Brisbane. Before that, I'd spent my time wholly on the coast, as far north as Rockhampton and Cairns in Queensland. I know it as well, almost, as any aborigine knows his own part of the interior. A lot depends, of course, on how well McRafferty knows it – or his First Mate. Have you any observations on that point?'

'None. I've no idea, beyond the fact they've both sailed to Australia for many years past.'

Graves nodded. 'I'll assume the First Mate, whats-isname —'

'Bullock.'

'I'll assume Bullock's taken pains to find out what he didn't already know. And if *I* wanted to land a man secretly along the east coast, it wouldn't be anywhere south of Brisbane.'

Halfhyde asked, 'What about the south coast – west of Sydney?'

Graves shook his head. 'Nowhere between Sydney and the Bight – if it was me, that is. None of the coastal areas apart from the towns and settlements are exactly populous down that way, certainly, but they're all too close to what passes for civilization in Australia and would in my view be hazardous. Queensland is different, so are Queenslanders. I'd hesitate to say they're lawless; but they certainly don't give a jigger for authority when authority gets uppish – if you follow. Also, Queensland does happen to hold more bad eggs than any other part. So that's where I'd make for.'

'Brisbane,' Halfhyde said reflectively. 'It was founded as a penal settlement, wasn't it?'

Graves chuckled. 'Yes, back in '25. The dust hasn't really settled yet – the feel's still there. It's a living illustration of what I've been saying, Halfhyde. Not that I'd suggest Brisbane itself. It's a very busy port, handling meat, hides, wool, tallow and country produce for export, cereals, soft goods and hardware for import. The mail boats run a monthly steamer service to Vancouver and Sydney, and the British India boats run an intermittent service to London, via the Torres Strait. No, I wouldn't choose Brisbane.'

'Where, then?'

Graves put the tip of his pencil on the chart and said, 'There. See? Walsh Island, in the lee of Cape Manifold. It's scarcely an island at all – the water's wadeable to the mainland. And it's very remote, totally uninhabited, yet at the same time your passenger wouldn't have all that far to go to reach the railway at Rockhampton. There's only one snag, one that shouldn't deter a good seaman too much – when the price is right!'

Halfhyde lifted an enquiring eyebrow and Graves said, 'The entry's tricky. Dangerous, in fact – very. McRafferty would need to pass through the Barrier Reef – here, through the Gemini Channel. It's not one of the recommended entries through the Reef, which is why I'd consider it suitable for a man who doesn't want his arrival known.'

Halfhyde pursed his lips. 'It makes sense, sir, but it's a long shot.'

'Oh, certainly, I'd agree. Bullock and his friend may have totally different ideas. All I've tried to show you is what *I* would do. But I'd take any wager you like that the man will be put ashore well north of Sydney and the closer to the Barrier Reef the more likely.'

'A large enough area! A large enough choice as well, for those who don't see with your own eyes, sir.'

Graves nodded. 'Yes. That's why I don't go so far as to suggest lying off outside the Gemini Channel and waiting for the *Aysgarth Falls* to sail up to us. What I do suggest is this: we make all possible speed direct for the coast, and then, having overhauled McRafferty by a wide margin, we steam to and fro across the track he'll most likely take for the whole area I've indicated. He'll have to start along that track when he's, let's say, two hundred miles off the coast, and I fancy I can narrow him down to no more than ten to twelve miles either side of the line. Now, what do you say, Halfhyde? It's a far better prospect – though I don't deny the long chance – than trying to seek McRafferty out through eight thousand miles of the Pacific!'

* * *

In the dark confines of the sail locker at night, Float ruminated long and hard. He'd got away with it this far; he'd even got away with the murder of the steward. That had been neat; a quick upward thrust with the knife and Goss hadn't had time to utter a word before he died. The disposal of the body – if there was no body, murder couldn't be proved and Goss could be considered to have fallen overboard, perhaps – had been easy enough. Goss was a small, skinny man; and McRafferty, on the poop, had stayed right aft throughout. The slight splash, no more than always resulted from the jettisoning of the ship's waste, had been covered by the hiss of water along the side and the rattle of blocks and other deck gear. It hadn't been the first time a dead man had gone unnoticed over the side of a ship at sea, after all . . . Float didn't rate it as anything big. Now the future loomed, and the turning of his night's exploit to the intended advantage to himself.

He had to find means of approaching the wealthy passenger: that was the next thing, the most important thing now. Float had no doubts in his mind that the passenger would prove amenable; he would have to be. Of course, there were dangers. Afterwards, Float would have a strong need to beat it fast. He didn't want to die at anyone's hands, the hangman's or otherwise.

Meanwhile he bided his time. No pushing things too far now. There were many days ahead; let fate decide, unless it looked like taking too long. In the event, it didn't take too long. Two more nights, and then the *Aysgarth Falls* met winds of gale force and the watch below, which included Float, was called out a little before midnight. McRafferty was tacking and the hands were required constantly to man the braces and haul the heavy yards round. When the force of the gale increased, the Captain decided to take the royals and topgallants off her and Float was one of those despatched aloft to the mizzen topgallant yard. Here he suffered a misfortune, as it seemed at the time: he missed the footrope and fell, screaming in terror. Grabbing wildly for a handhold on any rope that offered itself, he contacted one, slowed his fall but ripped the skin from his palm, and came down heavily, belly first, on the cro'jack yard just as the brace was hauled round. Float was dislodged, fell again, but managed to grab the shrouds on the starboard side just in time. He had fallen head first; his head took the bulwarks, but not too hard since his fall was to some extent broken by his grip on the shrouds, but enough to cause him to lose consciousness and drop, luckily inboard of the bulwarks, to the deck of the poop.

McRafferty dragged him to his feet. The head lolled but McRafferty didn't think the neck was broken. Cursing, McRafferty opened up the door at the head of the saloon ladder and bawled for his daughter. 'Float's injured,' he shouted. 'You'll not come up for him yourself, girl, but I have no hands to spare. Send Mr Jesson up. It's time the man had something to do – tell him it's an order and he's to waste no time.'

* * *

Float was not badly hurt; he was soon conscious again, left with a nasty headache, and the Captain's daughter soothing it with cold water and a sponge. She smiled at him; he gave her a grin and a wink. He'd never been so close to her before. Someone saw the wink: Jesson. Float became aware of him standing by the table.

'That's enough,' Jesson said. There was a smell of whisky, but Jesson, drunk or sober, was evidently the watchdog. Of course, the Old Man wouldn't risk his daughter alone with a murderer . . . Float said, 'Didn't do nothing, mister.'

'Keep it that way, then. You're scum. The lady's not to be insulted.'

The voice held authority, truculent authority, bullying. Float kept silent; then, as he began to feel better, he realized he had a kind of opportunity, one that had been handed to him on a plate, one that might never occur again. It was better to use it rather than have to force the issue later on when it might not be so easy. He thought for a while longer with his eyes shut; then

114

he opened them, stared at the girl, and said, 'Diamonds.'

He could almost feel the tension coming from Jesson. The passenger moved towards him, face suddenly white behind the beard. 'What was that you said?' he asked roughly.

'Diamonds, mister.'

'Why, you —'

'Eyes,' Float said dreamily, staring at Jesson. 'Miss McRafferty's eyes, like diamonds, shining in the light. Isn't that right, mister? Diamonds, worth a mint o' money. A real mint.'

'Shut your mouth,' Jesson snapped. There were red patches on his cheekbones now, just above the beard's growth. For a moment he stood in silence; the ship creaked and groaned around them, the decks canted sharply, the howl of the wind audible beyond the closed hatch and skylight. Jesson's mind had got there fast: Float, having just been warned not to get familiar with the Captain's daughter, would be unlikely to pay such compliments about eyes in Jesson's presence. Jesson had never had any reason to doubt his sergeant's ability to instil fear or to see to it that no order was disobeyed. Staring down at Float on the settee, he turned abruptly to the girl. He said, 'Leave us, Miss McRafferty.'

'He's still in need of attention,' she said.

'He's a murderer. He's wandering in the head – he may be dangerous, and I stand in for your father. Leave us.'

'Very well,' she said quietly, and went out of the saloon door. Jesson padded across after her and stood for a moment listening. When he heard her cabin door shut, he came back to Float. He said in a low voice, 'So it was you after all. You pried into my baggage. I thought as much, you dirty little scum.'

'Hard words break no bones, mister.'

'I wouldn't bank on not getting more than bloody words, Float.' Jesson breathed heavily, his hands clenching and unclenching. 'So it was you that killed Goss. You'll swing for that the moment I report to the Captain.'

'You'll report to no one,' Float said insolently, 'and me, I'm going to swing anyway so it makes no difference, does it? But it's the swinging I mean to avoid, mister, see?'

'You —'

'I opened one o' your cases,' Float said. 'Diamonds . . . talk about a bloody fortune, talk about fleshpots o' the East an' all that! Too much for one man, mister. Me, I got nothing.'

Jesson took another pace towards him, his face contorted. Float held up a hand, and rose to a sitting position. 'Watch it, mister,' he said. 'One touch and I'll yell for the girl and the Old Man. I'll tell 'em what you've got in your cabin, in them lovely cases. And then McRafferty, 'e'll tell the peelers in Sydney. McRafferty won't go much on it. McRafferty's straight, so I 'eard back in the Pool. I'm not, that's why they warned me.' Float gave a cackle of laughter. 'Don't you try nothing, mister. I bin done for G B H I 'ave and I'll bloody mince you up.'

He produced his knife, and held the blade towards Jesson, his eyes narrowed, as watchful as a rat.

'What do you want?' Jesson asked furiously. 'How much?'

Float said, 'That's not the main point. Maybe enough to help me on my way after —'

'You're not going anywhere, Float. Just to the gallows in Sydney, no further.'

Float grinned. 'That's just the bloody point,' he said. 'I'm not going to Sydney. I reckon you're not either – too many peelers an' that, too many questions. And I'm coming with you, see? Up to you to fix it with the Old Man. If you don't, then I opens me mouth like I said. Best see sense if you want all them diamonds to stay with you. And not go inside for hard labour the rest o' your life. Or swing yourself, maybe, but only you know about that.'

Jesson stood fuming, irresolute. Float grinned again and said, 'We're mates now, you an' me. Good mates. Both got something to lose. Stick together and we lose nothing, all right?'

He kept the knife steady.

There was murder clear in Jesson's face as Float got up and backed away towards the door of the saloon. Float saw it; he'd expected it and knew the risks. He said, 'Just don't try anything. Just don't.' Jesson, he reckoned, wouldn't try anything while the ship was at sea because for one thing he wouldn't get the chance: Float was watched all the time he was working on deck and when in the sail locker he was safe. Once they got ashore it would be different, but Float believed he could put his money on himself to strike first.

* * *

Jesson had a quiet word with Bullock next morning, on the poop, while McRafferty was below. He told the First Mate about Float.

Bullock's jaw came forward and his mouth set hard. 'That does it,' he said in a grating voice. 'I'm going to —'

'Wait,' Jesson said. 'You'll do nothing. For now, he's got us. See sense! It's not for long. Keep it all to yourself – all of it. For one thing: Float's not alone in this. Someone didn't lock him up that night after all —'

'Althwaite! I have his —'

'You won't, Bullock. You'll do nothing.' Jesson's voice was quiet but his stare into Bullock's eyes was intense and his grip on the First Mate's shoulder was hard. 'Nothing, I tell you. Except for just one thing.'

'And that is?'

'A word to McRafferty that I want to take Float with me when I leave the ship.'

'McRafferty'll never agree to that,' Bullock said flatly, 'so just cast it out of your reckoning.'

'It's got to be done, don't you understand?'

Bullock said, 'It can't be, you have my word on that. I know McRafferty well enough . . . and anyway, he's never going to put his head in that particular noose! What do they call it – compounding a felony, letting a murderer escape?' He shook his head. 'Best forget it. It won't work.'

Jesson licked at his lips, his eyes glittering through the mass of hair. 'I'm not blind to the difficulties, Bullock. They have to be overcome, that's all. There are other ways and well you know it.'

Bullock looked up sharply, not liking the tone. 'What are you getting at?'

'You know very well. Float.' Jesson drew a hand across his

117

throat, lifting the bearded chin and staring down his nose at the First Mate. 'Nothing so obvious as a knife, though. An accident.'

Bullock blew out his cheeks. 'You'll need to be careful.'

Jesson laughed. 'Not me, my good Bullock! You!'

'Me?' Bullock looked shaken.

'When do you think *I'*d have the chance for God's sake?' Jesson's eyes still searched the First Mate's face. 'It's got to be up to you. You've got the opportunities.' His voice hardened further. 'Don't forget you're in this deep, my friend. If anyone turns me in, you go with me.'

Bullock's face lost its colour. He said, 'All I did was fix your passage.'

'Yes. For a consideration extra to the passage money – remember? In hot diamonds. And I took the precaution of lodging your receipt in Her Majesty's mail, addressed to a good friend in Australia. Just bear it in mind.'

Jesson removed his hand from Bullock's shoulder and went below to the saloon. Savagely Bullock paced the poop, fists clenching and unclenching. It was clear enough that he had to go along with Jesson; there could be no half measures now. In any case it would be no more than a cheat upon the hangman; but the law wasn't going to take that line of argument! Desperately Bullock cast about for another way, a safer way, but couldn't see one. He would never persuade McRafferty; nor would he be able to get Float off the ship without McRafferty being aware when the time came. It was already going to be difficult enough to persuade McRafferty not to make his first landfall off Sydney Heads. Cantlow – Jesson – had left that to him as well; McRafferty, already worried about his passenger, certainly wasn't going to like such of the truth as he would need to be told.

When the moment came, McRafferty didn't. There was a row, and voices became raised in the apparent privacy of the saloon. The pressure was put on and McRafferty was forced to acquiesce. Working on the poop not far from the saloon skylight, Float was all ears . . .

TWELVE

If that overheard conversation was not proof enough that the First Mate was in with the passenger, Float, within the next day or so, found further evidence: Bullock was out to get him; not just to haze him, not just to make his life hell, but to do him in. Bullock was biding his time but seeking out every opportunity meanwhile. Working about the deck, Float felt Bullock's eyes constantly following him. In fair weather he wouldn't have much chance; but the moment a real blow came, Bullock's time would come with it. Any man out along the footropes was in danger and accidents not only could happen but did – all too frequently as this voyage had proved. And then there was the time spent in the sail locker. The First Mate naturally had access to the sail locker and might be crazy enough to do his killing during the night hours. Float didn't believe he would since a fall from aloft could be much more easily contrived but the fear stayed with him nevertheless. Without much hope he began praying for a nice, safe landfall.

* * *

From the *Tacoma* a watch was being kept for von Merkatz; but the seas astern remained empty of the German flag, much to Halfhyde's relief. As the days passed it seemed more and more unlikely that von Merkatz would pick them up again; though the German might well have overtaken them had it not been for their engines, since the wind had largely fallen away now.

There was also no sign of the *Aysgarth Falls*; as Graves

remarked, they could by this time have overhauled the windjammer and she might be to north or south of their course. He said, 'One more week and I believe she'll head up towards the Barrier Reef.'

Halfhyde nodded without commenting. He had not been entirely persuaded by Graves' reasoning. McRafferty could put his passenger ashore literally anywhere in Australia and the choice was in Halfhyde's view much too wide. He was growing more and more certain that they would never pick up the windjammer and that McRafferty would be left to carry the affair off in ignorance of how far he was committing himself. He said as much to Graves.

'It's up to him, after all,' Graves responded as they paced the deck outside the Master's accommodation. 'You're under no obligation to pull McRafferty's chestnuts from the fire.'

'Nor are you to deflect your ship, sir.'

'No.' Graves grinned. 'But, like you, I don't like to see it happen. We're both fools, I suppose.'

'Sentimental ones,' Halfhyde said, 'in regard to the wind-jammers . . . and the McRaffertys who work their guts out trying to keep them at sea.'

'The devil's own task.' Graves paused, looking sideways at Halfhyde. 'You said you'd go for steam when you buy your own ship – you're wise to do so. At the same time you'll forego a good deal of pleasure. There's nothing like sail, never will be.'

'I agree fully. But the windjammers are becoming less and less competitive every day, and I must be able to make a living.' He added dourly, 'I have a wife to support, at any rate when my father-in-law is not doing so. I prefer not to be under such an obligation, the more so when my father-in-law is my senior officer.'

'Indeed?'

'A vice-admiral, no less.'

'And his name?'

'Sir John Willard,' Halfhyde said.

Graves lifted his eyebrows. 'Willard! It's a small world to be sure —'

'You know him?'

'I don't say I know him. But I served under him three years ago when doing my time with the fleet. Malta . . . do I take it you married Miss Mildred Willard?'

'You may,' Halfhyde said.

'Ah.' The revelation seemed to end the subject; Graves coughed in some embarrassment, and the cough seemed to Halfhyde to be the only possible reaction to anyone having married Miss Mildred Willard. Graves returned to more nautical matters; Sydney, he said, if Halfhyde was ready to take the plunge, was a good place in which to find a likely steamer for sale and he, Graves, could provide some introductions.

'You forget, sir, I'm on articles to Captain McRafferty, and must sail home with him.'

'Always provided McRafferty and his ship have not been arrested by the authorities in Australia,' Graves said. 'If things rebound upon him, he'll be in serious trouble.'

'I shall still stand by his ship, sir.' Halfhyde looked up as a call came from the bridge. The Second Officer reported a steamer on the port bow, closing on a reciprocal course.

Graves went up the ladder, followed by Halfhyde. He said, levelling his telescope on the distant vessel, 'We may as well speak her. There's just a chance she's passed the *Aysgarth Falls*.' He added, 'That is, of course, if we've not overhauled her.'

* * *

The windjammer was in fact still a day's sailing ahead of the *Tacoma*; and dirty weather had come up the night before – the dirty weather that Float had been fearing. Once again it was a case of all hands. They swarmed aloft to get the canvas off, fighting the great sails to pass the buntlines. From the poop Captain McRafferty watched the helm, ready to pass instant orders as the wind howled and tore and the ship heeled far over to leeward. Seas swept the decks, foaming up against the hatch covers, submerging the windlass, rising over the fife-rails at the foot of the masts, green and cold and dangerous.

Bullock went aloft, racing his men up the foremast, up the futtock-shrouds and on to the foretopmast crosstrees and beyond. Float, sent to the fore upper tops'l yard, saw him coming, and, holding on with one hand, reached for his knife. The wind buffeted at him, invisible fingers bent on dragging him from the fragile safety of the footrope. Bullock, eyes gleaming in a fitful shaft of moonlight, came inexorably up the mast beneath. As he did so there came the agonizing sound of tearing canvas, then a crash as a yard was ripped free from the mizzenmast and fell in a tangle of rigging. McRafferty shouted from the poop.

'Mr Bullock, lay aft!'

Bullock took no notice. He climbed steadily. Float was alone on the yard. Float shook, and began to cry out; his voice was taken by the wind and flung to leeward. He mouthed in apparent silence, staring, unable to move. But he drew the knife and held it out towards Bullock's advance and began screaming imprecations, as unheard as his shouts for help.

Bullock had reached the yard now, was putting a boot out to take the footrope. The yard was canted sharply over to leeward and Bullock's advance was up hill. That gave Float some advantage; he stayed where he was, lips drawn back tightly against his teeth, his fist holding the knife steady. As Bullock advanced a wicked gust took the ship, which was labouring already; she went over further to leeward. More noise from aft indicated more gear going over; then there was a whipping sound from the fore royal mast as it reacted to the heavy list and the weight of the wind. By now the ship was in real difficulties, finding no help from her First Mate.

Bullock moved out along the yard staring fixedly at his quarry. Float moved backwards towards the yardarm, flailed at by the wind. Bullock came on, grinning now. He was mouthing something but Float couldn't hear what it was. Then a hand shot out and took Float's wrist like a vice, twisted it. The knife fell clear into the sea so many feet below.

Float gave a desparing shriek. Bullock let go of his wrist and lunged forward. Just as he did so the foretopmast stuns'l halliard parted; the 3½-inch hemp rope fell across the yard and Float shrieked again.

*   *   *

By next morning, when the *Tacoma* raised the steamer ahead on her port bow, the gale had blown itself out and only a confused swell was left behind. As the steamer closed, Graves took up his megaphone and altered course to bring his ship within hailing distance.

'Ahoy, there! What ship?'

The reply was bellowed back. 'SS *Werribee* out of Brisbane for Valparaiso.'

Graves gave the name of his own ship. 'Have you spoken the fully-rigged ship *Aysgarth Falls* out of Iquique for Sydney?' he called across.

There was some delay before the answer came back: the Master of the *Werribee* had not encountered the *Aysgarth Falls* herself but he had picked up a man cast overboard during a storm, clinging to a broken yard; and whilst in a state bordering on delirium the man had talked of the *Aysgarth Falls* – though on recovering he had denied all knowledge of such a ship.

Graves looked at Halfhyde, raising his eyebrows. Halfhyde said, 'This has the ring of mystery. It needs investigating more closely, sir.'

'You think it may be McRafferty's passenger?'

Halfhyde shrugged. 'We can but ask.'

Graves lifted his megaphone again. 'What is the man's name?' he called across the water.

'He refused to give a name, Captain.'

'I'll be damned,' Halfhyde said. 'I believe we must take this nameless gentleman over ourselves. Since we're also bound for Sydney, the castaway might as well avail himself of the opportunity to rejoin his ship!'

*   *   *

Float was lucky to be alive, for sharks had been around as the weather moderated. He had kept them off by making as much noise as he could, and the tangle of rigging that had gone over the side with the yard had helped to deflect their attacks. As he

123

sank into delirium sheer luck had come to his rescue: a fight had broken out between a cruising whale and the sharks, and they had left him, and then he had been sighted from the *Werribee*. Recovering in due course, he had panicked, refusing to answer the questions of the Master, asking repeatedly for passage home as a distressed British seaman. If pressed further, he would eventually give a false name; and he was beginning to feel some emerging sense of security when the ship was spoken by the *Tacoma*. The resulting sight of Halfhyde, who was pulled across to the *Werribee*, was a shock. Float did his best to persuade the *Werribee*'s Master that Halfhyde was up to no good and that he, Float, should remain untransferred. Halfhyde found little difficulty in persuading the Master otherwise. As a man facing a charge of murder aboard a ship at sea, Float was required in Sydney; the Master was indeed only too anxious to get rid of him once Halfhyde had put the facts before him.

Back aboard the *Tacoma*, Halfhyde asked questions and it all came out. Bullock had tried to murder Float, had tried to knock him from the yard, though in fact it had been the parted hemp that had finally done the knocking. Why had Bullock wanted to kill Float? Because, Float said, he knew too much.

'Tell me,' Halfhyde said.

Float did, vengefully. 'Diamonds,' he said. 'Bloody millions of them. That Jesson. The passenger.'

'I see. And you tried a little blackmail?'

Float said it wasn't blackmail, just that he'd said he'd talk if he didn't get assistance over a clandestine landing.

'Where does Captain McRafferty intend landing the passenger?' Halfhyde asked.

A look came into Float's eyes and he seemed to check what he had been about to say. After a pause he said, 'I dunno. Sydney, I reckon.'

'No, you don't, Float. You knew very well Captain McRafferty wouldn't land the passenger in Sydney – or rather, that the passenger would see to it that it wasn't Sydney. That was why you took the trouble to get a hold over him.'

'Well, maybe. But I don't know where he was to be put

ashore.'

'Think again, Float.'

'I said, I don't know.'

'I think you do, Float. And I also know why you're not admitting to it. You still have hopes of cheating the hangman, haven't you? Forlorn hopes as it happens – but still hopes. You should cast them from your mind, Float, and help me to nail the passenger.'

Float scowled: the last thing he wanted was for Jesson to be apprehended. Jesson knew that it was him, Float, who had killed Goss. Maybe Bullock had been told, but that would be simply hearsay and would remain so for as long as Jesson remained at liberty; and Float had it in mind that if the worst came to the worst and he was handed over in Sydney, he just might get away with manslaughter on the charge connected with the fire in the fo'c'sle. There had been a fight; tempers had been high – and the knife hadn't been aimed at the man who had died. Whilst shut up in the sail locker night after night, Float had had plenty of time for thought; many a murder charge had been reduced to one of manslaughter. Whilst in gaol himself, Float had come across more than one such case. It just depended on what sort of story you could concoct, how much of the gift of the gab you had, and how soft the judge was. But no amount of verbiage could ever get him off the hook of Goss – and Jesson had his tacit admission. Even if Float denied having made the admission, they would get there by taking all the known circumstances into account ... once Jesson had talked.

He said, 'I don't bloody know. No one told me. Jesson didn't know himself up to the time I talked to him. Or if 'e did, 'e didn't say.'

Halfhyde grunted, then turned away to stare from the port; the interview was being conducted in a spare cabin, with two hefty seamen outside the door. When Halfhyde had finished with him Float would be locked away below; but not yet. Halfhyde was convinced Float knew Jesson's landing place; that sudden flicker in the eyes had covered knowledge. It was vital that it should be dug out.

Halfhyde swung round. He said crisply, 'You no doubt learned aboard the *Aysgarth Falls* that I had served in Her Majesty's ships as a lieutenant. I still hold that rank, and the Master of this ship is a senior lieutenant of the Royal Naval Reserve. Also, you'll have seen the White Ensign.'

Float nodded, eyes alert and cautious.

'Very well, then. You'll understand that the *Tacoma* is now in effect commissioned as a warship. What do you know of the Navy, Float?'

'Little enough and don't want to learn more. Stuffed shirts, full o' bloody bull.'

'And dangerous to murderers, Float. Bear in mind that I was present when that man was knifed —'

'I didn't mean to —'

'I say you did, Float.' Halfhyde's voice was harsh, overbearing, and the look in his eyes matched his tone. 'Now I'll tell you something else,' he went on, tongue in cheek. 'The Captain of any of the Queen's ships has full authority to carry out the death sentence summarily if he believes it to be in the best interest of the service. Did you know that, Float?'

Float's eyes were wide, scared now. 'No. I reckon that only applies to mutiny.'

'Then where I am concerned you reckon wrong. A word to the Master and I shall have you hoist to the fore royal yardarm with a slack rope about your neck and a long drop to follow. Think about that, Float. I give you ten minutes.'

Halfhyde turned and stalked from the cabin. Climbing to the Master's deck, he found Captain Graves pacing up and down. Graves halted. 'Well, Halfhyde?'

Halfhyde grinned. 'A little softening-up, sir. I believe it will work.' He told Graves what he had said to Float. 'He may or may not believe my terrible exaggerations of a Captain's powers, but something tells me he believes that I personally am capable of anything – and he'll shrink from taking the risk!'

THIRTEEN

Float, the hands said, had got no more than he deserved. The feeling in the ship was lighter now; no one had liked a murderer aboard, a man destined only for the gallows. Better, as old Finney said, to let the sharks have him and put a quick end to it.

'They tears good,' he said to Althwaite. 'All them teeth. Mate o' yours, though . . . maybe I should 'old me tongue, eh.'

'No partic'ler mate,' Althwaite said. He was avoiding the taint: questions would be asked in Sydney about the disappearance of the steward and they might, just might, be directed towards any known friends of Float's if any suspicions were cast towards the man presumed drowned. 'We just come aboard together in the Pool, that's all. Chance, like.'

Finney said nothing further, just got on with his dinner: cracker hash, a foul enough mess but it stayed the hunger pangs with its crushed ship's biscuits, weevil-free with any luck, and its stewed bully beef. In the saloon, Bullock sat and ate the better fare of the afterguard along with the passenger and Miss McRafferty. Jesson kept eyeing the girl; he'd been at the bottle as usual, Bullock knew, maybe a little more than usual. Bullock hoped he would contain his nature and wait till he found an Abo woman on the coast. There wasn't all that long to go now and they didn't want any trouble on the last stretch. But Jesson would know that too; there was far too much at stake. As the meal drew to an end, attended by the cook acting as a makeshift steward, Fiona McRafferty, self-effacing as ever, excused herself and went to her cabin.

Jesson gave a belch. 'Pardon me. I held it in while the girl was here . . . always the gentleman. Right, Bullock?'

Bullock nodded.

Jesson fixed the cook with his eye. 'You. Get out.'

'That,' the cook said, 'is not the way a gentleman gives 'is orders. Not that you give orders to —'

Bullock interrupted. 'All right, Slushy. I'll give the orders instead. Back to the galley.' As the cook went out of the saloon looking murderous, Bullock looked at Jesson. 'Careful,' he said. 'Don't let the booze take charge. You're not in the clear yet, you know. It's still all up to McRafferty.'

'Talking of McRafferty . . . have you told him where I want to be put ashore?'

'Yes.'

'He's agreed?'

'Yes. He doesn't like it. That's why I'm urging caution. He could change his mind. Put a foot wrong and he will.'

'Meaning?'

Bullock said, 'I saw the way you were looking at the girl —'

'That's my business, Bullock.'

'Mine, too. I got you the passage . . . as you've reminded me more than once already. We're in this together, anyway till you're off the ship. And my advice is, lay off the girl.'

Jesson smiled nastily. 'Thank you for your advice, Bullock, but I don't need it. In fact, I bloody well object to it.' He lifted a bunched fist and brought it down on the table, hard. 'From now on, keep your advice to yourself, do you understand?'

'It's only in your own interest. You're a rich man, once you've landed all that stuff.' Bullock jerked a hand in the direction of Jesson's cabin. 'All the women you want, they'll be yours for the asking. Don't throw it all away. That's all I'm saying.'

Bullock got to his feet, picked up his peaked cap from the settee, and left the saloon. He went to his cabin for a couple of hours' sleep before taking over the watch from McRafferty. He found sleep didn't come easily; there was too much on his mind. All those diamonds . . . Float back there eastwards, disseminated into many sharks' stomachs. He'd got clean away with that, no questions asked thanks to the parting stuns'l halliard. Then there was Halfhyde, who could now be presumed dead thanks to the clearing house in Iquique. No one could ever fix that on him, that was sure. Halfhyde and his perishing Queen's ships . . . he would never come between him and his hand-out from Sergeant Cantlow, the hand-out that even McRafferty was in blissful ignorance of.

Sleep at last drifted down on Bullock's eyelids and they closed. He came awake again on the instant as a girl's scream tore through the bulkhead of his cabin.

* * *

Aboard the *Tacoma*, which was gradually overhauling the windjammer but passing well north of the latter's course, Float had suffered torment. He had taken his allowed ten minutes and then Halfhyde had come for him, together with four seamen, one of whom carried a length of rope over his shoulder. Halfhyde stood in the doorway, looking down at Float.

'Well?'

'Sod you,' Float said viciously. He stared at a blue-covered book in Halfhyde's hand. 'What's that you got there, then?'

The book's title could not be seen by Float: it was in fact the Admiralty Sailing Directions for the north-east coast of Australia. Halfhyde said coldy, 'The Articles of War, Float.'

'What's them?'

'A summary of crimes committed aboard Her Majesty's ships – and their punishments. It's the custom to read them to the defaulter before the death sentence is carried out.'

Float's face was as white as a sheet now. 'Sod you,' he said again through clenched teeth. 'You won't do it!'

Halfhyde didn't argue further. He moved from the cabin doorway and the seamen came in. Their faces were set, as white as Float's. Float looked at them in mounting fear: they, at any rate, looked convinced. Looked as if they didn't like what they were going to have to see. Float shook, had to be dragged to his feet. His unshaven cheeks were a dirty grey now, rather than white. He was taken up on deck and the procession made its way for'ard. Float hung back at the foremast shrouds. He looked up; it was a long, long way to the royal yard. A long drop.

'Climb,' Halfhyde said, 'or you'll be flogged up. With a cat o'nine tails, Float. I shall send for it if necessary.'

Float gave a whimper and climbed. He was shaking so badly that he had to use the lubber's hole rather than scale the futtock shrouds to the foretop. There was a formal grimness about Halfhyde that was terrifying and belief was fast settling into Float's mind. He clung on, stuck fast, feeling faint.

'Climb,' Halfhyde said behind him.

Float climbed on again. He was halted at the heel of the royal mast and the noose was placed about his neck; he felt the bulk of the hangman's knot as it fell against his chest.

'Climb,' Halfhyde said grimly. 'Not far now, Float.'

Float reached the royal yard and clung desperately to the narrow mast.

'Out along the yard to starboard.'

Float whimpered and looked down. He met Halfhyde's eye, saw the men below him. Tears streamed down his face. He said, 'God, you bloody mean it! You bloody *mean* it, don't you!' He clung to the mast's safety, grovelling now. 'Christ, take me down, I'll tell you what I know, *just take me down!*'

* * *

Graves looked at Halfhyde in some awe; the face was still formidable. Graves asked, 'Tell me, Halfhyde: would you have done it?'

Halfhyde laughed. 'Not unless I'd wished for a court-martial, to which even a half-pay officer is still liable! That's the truth of it – *now*. Up to the time he broke, I meant it. I *had* to mean it in order to convince.' He shrugged. 'If it had come to the point . . . I wonder!'

'I think you may have been in danger of convincing yourself, and could not have drawn back in time.' Graves was himself in a sweat of relief; as Master, he had been in some danger himself and wondered now if he would have stopped the terrible charade in time by a shout aloft. He mopped at his face.

'However, it appears to have worked, I gather. Where's the landing place to be?'

Halfhyde said, 'A look at the chart, sir, if you please.'

'Of course. Was I right?'

'Not entirely, sir. Cantlow's bound for Queensland, but not as far north as the Gemini Channel.' Halfhyde smiled as he followed Graves to the chart-room. 'As it is, we have the landfall very precisely now.'

* * *

Bullock came out of both his bunk and his cabin at the rate of knots. The scream had been desperate, terrified. It was no alarm resulting from an encounter with a ship's rat, a tailed and four-footed one ... Bullock was in time to see the passenger running from the girl's cabin, his clothing awry. At the same time McRafferty came down the ladder from the poop, his face furious in the light of the lantern coming from the open saloon door.

'What's all this, Mr Bullock?' Then McRafferty saw Jesson. Nothing more needed to be said. The clothing told its own story. 'Go to my daughter, Mr Bullock, see that she's cared for. I'll be in directly.'

'Sir, I —'

'Do as you're told, Mr Bullock, and don't delay. I shall see to this man.'

Bullock pushed past. McRafferty and the passenger faced each other. Both were breathing heavily. McRafferty said, 'You will stay where you are, and wait.' He turned towards his cabin but was halted by Jesson's harsh voice.

'She wanted it, you fool. You can't keep a young girl in purdah like the —'

'Shut your mouth!' McRafferty's face suffused with blood and he took a pace forward. 'You – scum! You filthy scum, to say a thing like that.' Once again he turned away for his cabin, moving fast. Jesson followed, a little unsteady on his feet, banging into the alleyway bulkheads on either side as he went. As he reached the Master's cabin door, he had his revolver in his hand. Hearing his entry, McRafferty swung round, bringing something from his safe: his own revolver, as carried by all shipmasters at sea for the ultimate preservation of discipline and authority. He saw the revolver in Jesson's hand and fired on the instant, taking the passenger before he could react. The bullet smacked into the heavy metal of the revolver, tearing it from Jesson's hand. Jesson stared at pouring blood, then looked up at McRafferty. 'All right,' he said softly. 'You've asked for it. Now you're going to get it.'

He advanced into the cabin, disregarding the gun in the Captain's hand. McRafferty took aim. At that moment Bullock came into the cabin, took it all in, and grabbed Jesson round the body, pinioning his arms. He spoke to McRafferty. 'It's all right. She's fine. Nothing happened.' He lurched about as Jesson struggled in his arms. 'She got the best of it. Let's just leave it be. There's been enough men lost for one reason or another.'

McRafferty stared back at Bullock and Jesson. In a tired voice he said, 'All right, Mr Bullock.' He laid the revolver aside, then walked up to Jesson. Lifting a fist, he hit with all his strength at Jesson's jaw. The head sagged and blood ran down the face. Breathing hard, McRafferty said, 'Put him in his bunk, Mr Bullock, and leave him to sober up. From now, there will be no more drinking – it is to be locked in my cabin. And we keep our course for Sydney after all.' He bent and picked up Jesson's revolver. 'I shall take charge of this.'

* * *

Next morning Halfhyde aboard the *Tacoma* was woken soon after the dawn had come up: a messenger sent down from the bridge was shaking him. The Officer of the Watch had sighted smoke on the horizon to the north-east. The smoke had grown slowly and then the vessel herself had come partially into view and had been identified from her fighting tops as a warship.

Halfhyde tumbled out of bed and went fast to the bridge, where Captain Graves had also arrived. Graves said, 'She could be German. A German cruiser – there's a too familiar look, though not much is visible yet.'

'Not von Merkatz again!'

'It's possible. You said he was persistent.'

'Then I was guilty of an under-statement, sir. The man's obsessed.'

Graves laughed. 'You did him some further damage, don't forget! No doubt that alone has redoubled his feelings of revenge.'

Halfhyde was looking through a telescope. 'It's him right enough,' he said after a while. 'Presumably he's felt able to leave his squadron to their own devices after all. The damage may not have been extensive.'

'And us?'

Halfhyde said, 'As before, sir. All possible speed – and hope to cross into Australian territorial waters before von Merkatz reaches us!'

'Well,' Graves said, 'let's hope your White Ensign can still hold his guns off, for he'll be within range in an hour or two's time.'

Halfhyde snapped his telescope shut, broodingly. He paced the bridge, backwards and forwards, his long jaw thrust out at a pugnacious angle. Von Merkatz looked as though he had the bit between his teeth and would not be deflected. Capture loomed. And what about McRafferty? Angrily Halfhyde wondered why he had bothered: let McRafferty stew! It was his own fault, as Graves had said. Yet Halfhyde knew he was unable to stand aside; there was always the nag of loyalty, a loyalty that he had felt even for the outrageous Captain Watkiss, RN. Watkiss, to whom all persons had been fools and idiots but who was the biggest bouncing fool of them all with his bombastic approach, his hidebound view of foreigners, his monocle, his large stomach and his short legs that on foreign service had been customarily encased in the longest white shorts that Halfhyde had ever seen; Watkiss, whose only reading matter apart from the seniorities in the Navy List had been Burke's *Peerage* and *Landed Gentry* – and woe betide an officer who was not included in one or other of them . . . if Halfhyde could be loyal to Captain Watkiss, then Captain

McRafferty whose ship was his whole life had every possible claim.

Halfhyde remained on the bridge, handy in case anything should happen. After an hour's steaming, von Merkatz had come no closer. It seemed he was simply shadowing. Halfhyde wondered what his purpose might be if that was the case. At the very least it seemed to indicate that von Merkatz was not going to be deterred by any consideration for the niceties of anyone's territorial waters. And he was going to be an infernal nuisance to say the least if he was still there when the clash came with Bullock and Sergeant Cantlow.

There seemed little prospect of deflecting him now. Even if the weather closed in . . . if it did that, then von Merkatz would close in too.

FOURTEEN

McRafferty was adamant that the passenger would be landed nowhere else but in Sydney.

'You're already involved,' Bullock pointed out angrily. 'It's in your own interest, Captain, to avoid the law.'

McRafferty shrugged. 'As to that, I must take what comes. I shall not become deeper involved, Mr Bullock, and Jesson must take it or leave it. If he cares to go overboard when we close the coast, and take his chance against the sharks, then he's welcome to do so and good riddance to him! I wouldn't see him go, and I wouldn't make any report to the authorities in Australia of my suspicions. But I *would* report that I had had a passenger who appeared to have fallen over the side. After that, they could make what they liked of it.'

Bullock looked shrewdly at McRafferty. 'Jesson's a rich man. He'd be prepared to increase the passage money.'

'From shady sources of income. Do you happen to know anything more precise about those sources, Mr Bullock?'

'I told you,' Bullock said truculently, 'I don't know any more than you do now.' The diamonds had not been mentioned to McRafferty; according to Bullock's story Jesson had simply had some unknown contretemps with the law in a South American state and had needed an urgent passage out of Chile. Bullock had only been the go-between and he hadn't questioned Jesson too far: his money was good and it had been in cash. Bullock said, 'Of course, he's in your hands . . . I've no doubt I can put the squeeze on. After all, he's there to be milked.'

McRafferty said, 'I'll not help any further, Mr Bullock, after what happened. The man's nothing but a rogue and I'd be glad enough to see him behind bars.'

'But your involvement —'

'I have said my last word on the matter, Mr Bullock, and our course is for Sydney Heads. As to my involvement, I may decide to meet any difficulty by ensuring that the man's handed over to the authorities.' McRafferty turned away; the conversation had been held at the fore rail of the poop, out of earshot of the helmsman. McRafferty went aft, hands behind his back and his face formidable. Bullock stared after him with a grim expression, then moved away for'ard and began shouting at the hands to ease his temper and his frustrations. Something would have to be done, but what? Maybe Jesson would have some ideas on the point.

* * *

Von Merkatz remained at his chosen distance behind the *Tacoma*, not closing, not falling back. As the days passed towards the Australian landfall, he was ever there, their constant companion. There was no exchange of signals between the ships; they might have been total strangers, merely following the same course. Halfhyde lifted a telescope towards the German cruiser, as though even a distant sight of the ship could give him some clue as to what von Merkatz intended to do. The German would face any amount of difficulties if he continued the chase, not least among them a need to watch his bunkers. Coal didn't last for ever; and it might be possible, if the naval authorities at Garden Island in Port Jackson could be contacted and told a thing or two, for bunkering facilities to be refused in all Australian ports. Then von Merkatz would be in a nasty jam, with much to explain away to the German naval command in Kiel. And what, in all conscience, could he hope to do about achieving his objective of getting Halfhyde aboard his ship? Most certainly the Australian authorities would not connive at that, and once the *Tacoma* was in port . . . on the other hand, if the coast of Queensland offered anonymity to

McRafferty's passenger and his haul of diamonds, then it also offered a high degree of opportunity to von Merkatz in regard to his own quarry.

Halfhyde lowered the telescope, snapped it shut and turned to Graves. He said, 'I believe you may be standing into danger, sir.'

Graves cocked an eye at him. 'You don't mean navigationally, of course.'

'Yes.' Halfhyde put forward his anxieties about the area of the Brisbane River and the southern fringes of the Great Barrier Reef. 'I would put nothing past Admiral von Merkatz —that's where the danger lies. If it suits his purpose, he'll not hesitate to put your ship in hazard off the Reef.'

Graves laughed. He said in mock reproof, 'You, of course, never once thought of doing the same thing to his ships!'

'*Touché!*' Halfhyde returned the smile. 'But at least I'm British!' he added, tongue in cheek.

'A somewhat chauvinistic sentiment, surely?'

'Yes. It's a legacy from one Captain Watkiss under whom I served on a number of different occasions. Captain Watkiss was a very patriotic officer, one who often expressed his view that it was unfortunate that foreigners couldn't all be British. I confess I often found myself appreciating his point.'

* * *

Bullock had had a word with Jesson. Jesson was not going to be taken to Sydney; he was putting his head into no noose. 'Try McRafferty **again**,' he said. 'I'm willing to pay more.'

'I've told him that. It's no use. He's made up his mind and that's that. There's no one more obstinate than McRafferty when he wants to be.'

'Right, then,' Jesson said harshly. 'There's only one thing we can do, isn't there?'

Bullock looked at him narrowly. 'What's that?'

'You take the ship north for Queensland.'

'How?'

Jesson snapped, 'By taking over command.'

'I can't do that!'

'You can if I say so,' Jesson said.

'Only by using force on McRafferty. And once I do that, I'd never get another berth. No, you can count me out.' Bullock spoke with determination. 'I'm not taking part in anything that involves actual force, so help me God! You'll have to think of another way.'

Jesson sneered. 'You're yellow, Bullock.'

'Just prudent. You're not paying enough to keep me the rest of my life, you know.'

'Why not come in with me, leave the sea?'

Bullock shook his head. 'You'd not stick to that sort of bargain once we were ashore. I'm no use to you after that and I know it. So do you. Anyway, without McRafferty we might never make it. They're tricky waters off the Barrier Reef.'

'Lost your self-confidence, Bullock?'

Bullock shook his head. 'It's not that. It's that you need more than just one man who knows what he's about, aboard any ship, anywhere, let alone off the Reef. McRafferty's needed and you'd best not forget that. To put it at its simplest . . . we've a while yet to go and I can't do watch on, stop on all that time and still be wide awake when it comes to a difficult job of navigation and ship handling.'

Jesson nodded, slowly and thoughtfully. 'That makes sense, I suppose. Well, there's got to be another way, that's all. And there is. And this time I don't want any of your damned objections, Bullock. Because if you don't go along with me I just might decide that I can't stand the sight of you any longer.' He reached into a pocket and brought out a revolver. 'McRafferty doesn't know I carried two guns, Bullock. I'll use this the moment I see the need. Now, just you listen to me.'

*　*　*

There was no knock at the door of the girl's cabin: a man entered, grinning, with a revolver aimed and Fiona McRafferty gave a sharp cry.

'Keep your mouth shut,' Jesson said in a low voice. He was

138

across the cabin in an instant and had pressed a hand over the girl's lips, tightly. With his free hand he pushed the snout of the revolver into her side. 'One sound and I'll shoot. Then I'll shoot your father when he comes down from the poop.' He paused. 'I hope you've got that, Miss McRafferty, because I'm going to let go of you now and by God if you don't do as I said and keep quiet, you'll make the last sound you'll ever make. Understood?'

She nodded. Jesson let go, then indicated the bunk. 'Lie down on it,' he said. She did so. From beneath his jacket Jesson produced five lengths of codline, thin but strong. Looping a length round ankles and wrists, he tied the girl down to the bunk; the fifth length went round her mouth and a twisted curtain that Jesson had removed from his cabin port. It made an effective gag. This done, Jesson stood back. He said, 'Just behave, that's all, and you'll be all right.' She stared up at him and he laughed at the fear in her eyes. 'Don't worry . . . I won't be having the opportunity for what you're thinking, Miss McRafferty. There's other business afoot for now and I'll not be taking any chances. If you're worried about your father, well, he'll be all right too, so long as he does what Bullock tells him.'

Jesson sat down, on a chair near the bunk. He kept the revolver in his hand. He waited. Up top on the poop, by the fore rail, Bullock was talking to McRafferty in a quiet but threatening voice. McRafferty, finding difficulty in believing his ears, nevertheless held himself in check. Bullock was convincing. And what Bullock said had struck at the very roots of his being. Everything he possessed was under threat. Bullock said that if he uttered a word out of place to the crew, or if the crew got wind of the facts and acted in a way Jesson didn't like, or if McRafferty didn't take the *Aysgarth Falls* up towards the Barrier Reef . . . if he didn't act naturally as a shipmaster in full command . . . then his daughter would suffer. So would his ship, his home. It would be the easiest thing in the world to pile her up along the Reef, with Jesson already away in one of the ship's boats, and let her smash to matchwood in the seas that would pour across the coral in the first bit of bad weather to hit the Queensland coast. It had, Bullock said, to be a case of best foot foremost, all the rest of the way.

'You're scum, like Jesson, Bullock.'

'I have to think of myself, Captain.'

'What do you get out of it?' McRafferty asked bitterly. 'Beyond a bullet in the back the moment you're ashore with Jesson?'

'I shan't go with him,' Bullock said.

'Because you know the risks. What about me? Do I land Jesson and then sail on for Sydney as though nothing had happened? Do I let you get away with it, or do I turn you in the moment we make the berth at Sydney? Do you see no risk in that . . . or do you intend to kill me once your filthy business with Jesson is finished?'

Bullock didn't answer directly. He said, 'Just do as you're told. Do that, and no one's going to get hurt. You won't make matters better for yourself by doing anything that Jesson doesn't like. One more thing: when you go below, keep clear of your daughter's cabin. And I want the key of your safe – I'll come down with you.'

'You mean you want my revolver.'

'Yes,' Bullock answered. With McRafferty he walked aft for the saloon hatch. McRafferty seethed but knew when he was beaten; his daughter couldn't be put at any further risk. Nor could his ship. There was nothing at all that he could do. After handing his revolver to Bullock, he went back to the poop, doing his best to appear normal in the view of the helmsman and the fo'c'sle hands working about the deck. He paced, long training and his seaman's instinct ensuring that he kept a sharp eye on the set of the sails and the proper handling of the wheel. As he paced he tried to make some assessment of the fo'c'sle crowd, tried to see which way they would go if they got the word that the Master was no longer in control of the ship. If he could have trusted them, he might well have mustered help. A rush below could possibly catch Jesson out in time for Fiona to be saved from harm; on the other hand the ladder and the alleyway were narrow and the men wouldn't be able to advance on a broad front, no hope of surrounding Jesson. In any case, old Finney apart, the trusted men were gone: the bosun, the carpenter, the steward, Halfhyde. As for the rest, they were a ragbag, some of whom had sailed with him before, some of whom had not. Of those who had not he knew little beyond their seamanship abilities or lack of them as revealed on passage from the Mersey. But McRafferty knew seamen, as such, well enough: apart from a few solid hands whose honesty and integrity shone from their faces, the men who sailed before the mast would take any chance to do down an owner so long as it looked profitable to themselves; and were always basically against authority in the shape of the afterguard. When it came to the point they might turn to Jesson – certainly would if the man shared his spoils with them.

But Jesson wouldn't want to do that. Wouldn't want them to know too much of his business.

McRafferty's only hope, as he saw it, lay in that.

Broodingly, he paced on. In due course Bullock came up to take over the watch, and McRafferty went below to the saloon. Meaning to break his own rule of abstinence at sea, he took a key from his pocket and approached the locked cupboard containing the Dunville's whisky. He found the lock broken and the whisky gone: Jesson had been there before him.

McRafferty's fears for his daughter mounted. He remained wakeful in the saloon, dreading to hear a cry from the girl's cabin. He heard nothing, and found the total lack of sound as unnerving as a cry would have been. After half an hour he could stand his inactivity no longer. He got to his feet and went through the door of the saloon, into the alleyway, moving softly towards Fiona's cabin. Still no sound. McRafferty reached out for the doorhandle and very slowly turned it. He pushed. The door didn't move. Of course, Jesson had locked himself in, that was to be expected. But locks could be broken by the impact of a heavy shoulder. McRafferty hesitated; one blow might not do it, and before he could smash the door open his daughter might suffer.

Looking defeated, he turned away. Then he heard the door come open behind him, and he turned back. He stared into the muzzle of Jesson's revolver. Jesson was grinning like a devil.

141

'You move about like a rhinoceros, Captain. Try the handle again and you know very well what'll happen. Now vamoose before the girl gets it.'

* * *

During the next few days the *Aysgarth Falls* met adverse winds; all hands were kept busy on deck and on the footropes, and progress through the water was slow. By now McRafferty, in obedience to Jesson's wishes, was bringing his ship up northerly to make the new landfall between the Barrier Reef and the mouth of the Brisbane River. The windjammer's slowed progress was allowing Halfhyde aboard the *Tacoma* to steam well ahead and by the time fifteen days had passed since the renewed sighting of von Merkatz the steamer had raised the Queensland coast ahead, with the Brisbane River and its busy shipping routes well to the south.

When the report was sung out by the masthead lookout Graves and Halfhyde were on the bridge. Both looked ahead through telescopes; it was a while before the coast came into view from their lower level; and shortly after it had done so, Graves said, 'That's it.' He waved a hand towards the starboard bow as he lowered his telescope. 'Do you see it, Halfhyde?'

'See what in particular, sir?'

'Breakup Island.'

Halfhyde took a long look; the forebodingly named Breakup Island had been the place reported by Float as Jesson's disembarkation point. The landfall had been a splendid one. Graves had once again brought up his telescope. 'No sign of the windjammer, Halfhyde. She must be astern of us, as I expected.'

'Yes. The auguries seem a shade better!'

Graves nodded. 'So long as our presence doesn't drive McRafferty away when he gets here.'

'We shall give chase, sir. And no one aboard the *Aysgarth Falls* will be expecting *me* to be aboard, with full knowledge of Jesson - nor will they suspect the presence aboard us of the good Float.'

'True enough, but what about von Merkatz?'

Halfhyde swore. The German was still in attendance, still keeping his station as the *Tacoma* made in towards the distant coastline. 'As ever, the Hun nigger in the British woodpile – but one that has to be accepted.'

'What do you propose to do about him?' Graves asked again.

Halfhyde gave a short, hard laugh. 'At this moment, I have no idea. I suggest a masterly inactivity in regard to von Merkatz until such time as I'm struck by a stratagem.'

Graves said, 'Somehow I doubt if he'll be prepared to be disregarded. I think we'd do well to enter Australian territorial waters, Halfhyde. The protection may be slight enough, but it's all we can do.'

Halfhyde nodded thoughtfully. 'It's a desolate coast. No one to witness anything.'

'Which is why your passenger chose it.'

'Yes, indeed! It's admirably suited to von Merkatz' purposes of attempting to remove me —'

'You think he'll really do that?'

'I'm certain he will, sir, and we shall need to take evasive action, with your permission. If he opens fire I shall quit your ship – but I'm hopeful he won't do *that* at any rate, once we enter Australian waters.' Halfhyde paused. 'Suppose, then, we run for Breakup Island, so as to be on station when the *Aysgarth Falls* makes her landfall – and that we remain hidden from her around the inshore side, and chance what von Merkatz may do? A look at the chart —'

'Shallow water on that side —'

'Exactly, sir. Enough for us, not enough for von Merkatz and his heavy cruiser. Shall we proceed inwards, sir?'

Graves said, 'I'm agreeable to that – but what about the man Jesson? When he sees a man-o'-war laying off —'

'I've given that some thought too. But I think we must regard first things first, and see to our own temporary security – Captain McRafferty may be days astern of us yet for all we know. In the meantime something may occur to help us, though I'm far from hopeful of that.'

They watched out ahead as the *Tacoma* approached the coast. There was a strong on-shore wind from the east now; soon they could see the long rollers pounding the coastline, raising a heavy spray; and soon after that they were able to hear, distantly, the booming roar of the rushing waves as they washed the lonely beaches. Behind them von Merkatz steamed on with his great turreted batteries. Halfhyde paced the *Tacoma*'s bridge, frowning, cudgelling his brains. Von Merkatz, thwarted by the lack of depth to take his ship close to Breakup Island, might well decide to put a landing party ashore to prevent Halfhyde's escape to the mainland, or he might make another and easier attempt to board the *Tacoma*. In either event, the British seamen, unarmed but for the Master's revolver in his cabin, would be unable to fight back against a naval guard armed with rifles and bayonets.

Halfhyde's face was glum as the *Tacoma* moved on and Graves pointed her bows towards a narrow channel that led through dangerous shoals to Breakup Island, a grim-looking place in its own right, desolate, barren, uninhabited, with some rising ground in rear that had a look as though in time it was going to be washed clean away by the action of the waves.

* * *

As night came down the steamer was hove-to, hidden away behind the lee of Breakup Island and Halfhyde reckoned she would be invisible from the *Aysgarth Falls* when the wind-jammer made her arrival. But the worries had by no means lessened. At any moment German attack might come if von Merkatz decided to risk entry. Even if it did not, the point made earlier by Captain Graves was a very valid one: when Jesson saw the warship, he would insist that McRafferty turned away seawards again. If the windjammer was sighted in time from the *Tacoma*'s lookout now stationed at a vantage point on the island's high ground, Halfhyde could follow out to sea and make contact. But to leave Breakup Island the *Tacoma* would have to steam slap into von Merkatz. It was anyone's guess as to what might then happen.

'Win, or lose it all,' Halfhyde murmured.

'What's that?'

'Mere reflections of a harrassed mind, sir. The only way to success now is to get rid of von Merkatz and his confounded cruiser. And I believe I'm beginning to see daylight. The risks will be great, I don't deny – and it's unfair to ask for your assistance. There will be no hard feelings on my part if you don't wish to risk your ship.'

'What have you in mind?' Graves asked.

Halfhyde laid a hand on his shoulder. 'The chart, sir. Let us take a close look at the chart and the Admiralty "Pilot". I noticed that there is another entry channel to Breakup Island, and another entry means another exit at the same time.'

Graves blew out his cheeks. 'Good God! Are you referring to Disaster Passage by any chance?'

'Yes, sir, I am. Let us take that look at the chart.'

* * *

All hands were at their stations as dusk came down. Graves had agreed to move out, though with reluctance. He had made the exit through Disaster Passage once before, when Mate of a pearling vessel that had had to sail at a time when a disabled wool ship had drifted towards Breakup Island and had gone aground in the main channel and blocked the narrow fairway. Disaster Passage was well named, he said: ships never used it if it could be avoided. So far as he knew, he and his former shipmates had been the only seafarers to use it almost within living memory. He said, and this was confirmed by the Sailing Directions, that its name derived from the fate of a barquentine that had tried to make the passage some seventy years earlier. Her master and crew had been overpowered by escaped convicts who had seen a direct run out by sea as being their best bet. There had been a government cutter patrolling out from the Brisbane River so they had decided to use Disaster Passage to elude its attentions in much the same way as Halfhyde meant to elude von Merkatz: Disaster Passage would take them out to sea well south of the proper entry and exit channel outside which von Merkatz was lying. Those convicts had never come out from the Passage; their bodies, and those of the barquentine's crew, had eventually been found still aboard the vessel which had piled up on some jagged rocks. There had been indications that the men had prepared to swim to the mainland with such possessions as they had with them; but they had been attacked first. Their wounds had been appalling; and the theory was that they had been set upon by Aborigines in enough strength for the whole lot to be slaughtered to a man. 'I can tell you,' Graves said, 'we were all praying last time I went through.'

'We shall pray again,' Halfhyde said. He intended taking upon himself the task of going away in a ship's boat ahead of the steamer with a lead and line, to take soundings and call back directions to Graves; and he was about to embark and be lowered to the water when there was a shout from the lookout, now withdrawn from the island and positioned at the crosstrees below the fore royal mast.

'Boat in sight, sir!'

'What's her heading?' Halfhyde called back, cupping his hands.

'Entering the channel, sir, with a party aboard. I reckon they're Huns, sir.'

Halfhyde grinned through gathering dusk at Graves. 'It's time we were away, sir!'

'And if we're spotted?'

Halfhyde shrugged. 'It's in the lap of the gods now.' He turned for the ladder and went down fast towards the boat's falls. As he did so there was another shout from the fore royal mast: the boat was coming round the island and was making no attempt to put men ashore. That looked as though von Merkatz intended to board direct. It also meant a stern chase, which would be far from funny in the dangerous shoals that dotted Disaster Passage.

FIFTEEN

As the *Tacoma* got under way in increasing darkness there was a shout in German from astern followed by the crack of a rifle when the shout was unanswered. After that there was no more firing; it semed likely that the German had settled for no more than a shadowing manoeuvre, as von Merkatz had done across half the Pacific Ocean already. Halfhyde, constantly casting his lead line from the boat ahead, reflected that von Merkatz was showing an unusual sensitivity: he seemed to have no desire to flaunt international practices too far, at any rate not to the point of keeping up a constant rifle fire to harrass the British ship's crew.

After a while the German boat withdrew, which was even stranger. Halfhyde puzzled over the matter: why send the boat in the first place? Then he reflected that when he had sent the boat off, von Merkatz wouldn't have known the *Tacoma* was getting under way. The fact that she had now been seen to be moving into Disaster Passage was enough, no doubt, for von Merkatz. He would refer to his chart and then go to sea himself, waiting off the exits farther south for his quarry to reappear.

Halfhyde swore to himself. There was no escape from a lion that merely moved to close the escape route. But all he could do now was to go on. There could be no turning back even if he wanted to. Heaving his lead line ahead again, waiting for it to come up-and-down as his boat moved on, Halfhyde sang out the depth of water. Behind him the *Tacoma* moved dead slow through the shoals and past the jags of rocks. There was a long way to go; there were several possible exits, some safer than others; they could take their choice. That aspect might be of some help in avoiding von Merkatz, who couldn't watch all the exits all the time. But that was a frail thread upon which to base any solid hope; von Merkatz, steaming up and down the coast, would be sure to sight them soon enough.

*　*　*

McRafferty was sunk by now in despair and the thought that he might never see his daughter again once Breakup Island was reached. It was a hundred pounds to a penny that the man would have ideas of using her in some fashion to cover his getaway from the *Aysgarth Falls*. And once away, he would have a fine start so long as Fiona remained the sanction against her father. It would not take the *Aysgarth Falls* long to reach Brisbane and lay the information, and McRafferty had intended to do this no matter how much trouble might come to him for his own part in the affair. But he would hesitate to speak if Fiona was with Jesson after the landing. Bullock, without being specific, had hinted that a hostage was in Jesson's mind; and McRafferty hadn't needed to be told that the first person to die if the net closed on Jesson would be the hostage and the incriminating knowledge in his or her mind.

He could find no way through his predicament; he was alone and he was powerless, a shipmaster who had lost control of his ship through the chicanery, to use no harsher a word, of his own First Mate. Naturally, Bullock would be finished so far as ever getting another berth at sea was concerned; but this would not restore McRafferty's loss. Bullock . . . disloyalty at sea was almost the worst of crimes on its own, in McRafferty's view. What Bullock fancied he might be gaining by his behaviour was beyond all comprehension; but no doubt, like himself, he had got in beyond his depth in the first place.

McRafferty paced the poop, his face grim. If only he had Halfhyde with him; but it was useless to think about that. Probably Bullock had had a hand in that as well, seeing Halfhyde as someone who would upset his schemes for an illegal landing of the passenger.

148

As McRafferty turned at the after end of the poop, a figure emerged from the saloon hatch and McRafferty called to him.

'Mr Bullock.'

'Aye, sir.' The niceties were still being observed; on the surface all was well between Master and First Mate. Bullock made his way aft, long arms swinging.

McRafferty said, 'A word in your ear.' He kept his voice low. 'Do you imagine you're going to get away with this?'

Bullock shifted his feet. He was clearly uneasy. McRafferty went on, 'You told me you didn't intend landing with Jesson. Tell me what you do mean to do with the rest of your life – that's if you don't swing for mutiny.'

'Mutiny . . .' Bullock rasped a hand over an unshaven chin. 'That's a strong word —'

'A right one, Bullock. Mutiny is what you did.'

'At the point of a gun. I had no option.'

McRafferty bristled. 'You had every option! If you admit to cowardice —'

'Cowardice is no crime. No court will ever say it was. And there was your daughter.'

'I think you were of little help to my daughter, Bullock. And then you uttered threats to me. Be assured that all the facts will see the light of day as soon as we berth in Sydney. I imagine you never doubted that they would. I imagine also that you may have it in mind to kill me before I can make those facts known. Am I right?'

Bullock scowled but gave no answer. McRafferty nodded as though he had received confirmation. He said, 'That's one thing you'll not risk, Bullock, dangerous to you as I may be. I believe Jesson won't risk it either —'

'Why's that?'

'Because I shall remain on deck from this moment until we finally enter our proper port of Sydney and make fast to the berth. It's a long stretch . . . but I've been forty years a seaman, Bullock, and it'll not be for the first time. There will always be some of the hands about and I shall be in full view. Neither you nor Jesson can make a clean sweep of the whole of my crew.' McRafferty paused. 'You have one chance, and one chance only.'

'And that is?'

McRafferty said, 'You're not under threat from Jesson's revolver while you're up here, and you have not been at any time since he entered my daughter's cabin. That gives you freedom of movement —'

'You forget your daughter, Captain.'

'I do not. But I believe there is a way to resolve the matter without her coming to any harm. It'll need your co-operation. That's what I'm asking for. If you give it, and if together with the crew we succeed, then there are matters that I shall find it conceivable to forget – or make no mention of to the authorities. Well?'

Bullock seemed about to make some answer when there was an interruption, a shout from the foretopmast head.

'Land-ho! Land fine on the starboard bow!'

Bullock snatched McRafferty's telescope from his hand and moved for'ard at the double, running for the foremast shrouds. He climbed nimbly, searched the distant shore-line, then came down. Moving aft, he approached McRafferty again. He said, 'We've made a landfall a little south of Breakup Island. There's no time to alter things now. What's done must stay.'

* * *

As dawn came up, thin and watery to herald a dirty day, Halfhyde hailed the *Tacoma* still moving on slowly behind him.

'How far to go now, sir?'

Graves glanced at the chart, spread before him on the steamer's bridge. 'I make it a little more than six miles,' he called back.

Halfhyde groaned and went back to his task of taking soundings. In point of fact Disasater Passage hadn't proved as bad as he had feared from the horrific account in the Sailing Directions; but it was utter desolation, almost terrifying in its loneliness, an excellent part of the coast to land a man on the run, so long as he could survive until he reached the outposts of civilization. Jesson, Halfhyde supposed, would equip himself with basic foodstuffs and fresh water from the *Aysgarth Falls*, but things could still go very wrong with him if he fell in with any hostile Abos. If he did, there would be justice in that. The boat was pulled on; the casting of the lead line continued. Halfhyde was cold and wet; there had been a thinnish rain for the last three or four hours and now it was coming down harder, penetrating even the oilskins worn by the boat's crew, trickling down the necks and up the sleeves as they pulled on the oars. The surroundings were dreary: greenish water, with a surf coming over the shoals, the mainland grey and dismal and half obscured by the weather. Clouds hung low and there was little wind to move them. Halfhyde shivered; it would be a depressing place in which to die and he spared another thought for the unlucky convicts on the run so many years before. Convicts so called – men who had taken bread to feed their families were said to have outnumbered the real criminals. Harsh days; the men who had died aboard that barquentine had very probably been far better men than Sergeant Cantlow alias Jesson.

The rain was worsening . . . Halfhyde was reminded of his honeymoon, as much a misnomer as to call hungry men convicts. It had rained in Scotland and to be confined indoors had brought no solace. Even if Mildred had been disposed towards consummation of the marriage, she would have bridled at such a thought in daytime. It would not be seemly; the cloak of darkness was more respectable. The boat trip across Loch Lomond had taken place during a bright day when the mists had vanished, but it had been damp, and Mildred had complained about the boat's thwarts transferring the moisture to what she referred to as her sit-upon. Halfhyde grinned at the thought of his coarse response to that euphemism, which had been uttered with a blush, a very daring remark that he had hoped might have been intended to indicate a thaw. Not so; Mildred had become huffy and even more withdrawn and she hadn't spoken for the rest of the day. Halfhyde found himself hoping it was raining now in Portsmouth, or Newmarket if Mildred was there still. More than her sit-upon would be wet if she were riding, but then so long as a horse was available she didn't mind the weather ... Mildred had been born with the wrong form; she should have been a mare, but if she had would no doubt have galloped at speed from the sight of a stallion.

The water beneath the boat was deepening now, deepening fast, and the land was opening out towards the sea. Halfhyde was about to hail the steamer when he was himself hailed by Graves.

'We're through, Mr Halfhyde! All safe now.'

Halfhyde waved. 'I'll return and come alongside for hoisting, sir.' He paused. 'Is there any sign of von Merkatz outside, or the *Aysgarth Falls*?'

'No sign of von Merkatz, but there's a full-rigged ship coming into view from easterly. I can't identify her.'

Halfhyde waved again. The ship could be anything, making into the Brisbane River to the south, though it was doubtful if she would make her landfall quite so northerly if Brisbane was her destination. He let the boat drift as the *Tacoma* came up; the crew hooked on to the falls and the boat was hoisted and secured to the davits. Halfhyde made his way to the bridge.

Graves pointed out the sailing ship, still distant. Halfhyde studied her through a telescope. 'I believe it's Captain McRafferty, sir, though I can't yet be certain. If it is . . .'

'This is where the trouble starts,' Graves said. 'You can rely upon my assistance, Halfhyde.'

'Thank you, sir. I'm grateful. Now we must watch for von Merkatz.'

Graves said, 'He'll know nothing about the *Aysgarth Falls*. He'll not be taking any particular notice of her —'

'But she will of him if he emerges, as we said earlier. Once the cruiser's spotted, Jesson will see to it that the *Aysgarth Falls* fades away again to sea.'

'Von Merkatz won't follow, presumably?'

'No. For the same reason as we've just mentioned – she'll appear harmless enough so far as he's concerned. For us – I suggest we go astern a little way, sir, until we're hidden again by the land. We can keep a watch from the fore royal yard – there should be a clear view across the spit of land, I fancy.'

152

'And if the windjammer turns away —'

'Then I shall assume it's the *Aysgarth Falls* and that von Merkatz has been spotted. Captain McRafferty – or Jesson – shall be our distant lookout!' Halfhyde rubbed his hands together; there was the light of battle in his eyes now. 'If she turns away, we chase – and pray that we'll have a fair start on von Merkatz!'

SIXTEEN

Bullock had gone below to report the sighting of land to the passenger.

'Is it all clear?' Jesson asked from the cabin doorway.

Bullock nodded; he was unaware of the presence of the *Tacoma* and the German cruiser, both of them well concealed in the lee of Breakup Island. 'Not a ship in sight – so far,' he said. 'We're bound to pick up someone sooner or later, making in or out of the river.'

'I don't doubt that. Tell McRafferty he's to get in the lee of the land as fast as he knows how.'

'It's up to the wind,' Bullock said, and turned away. Then he turned back. 'How's Miss McRafferty?'

'She's all right. Are any of the hands getting nosey?'

'I don't think so,' Bullock answered.

'Get back on deck, then, and keep it that way. Just a moment, though, something you can do. Get along to my cabin and bring all my gear in here. All the leather bags.' Steel came into the voice. 'All of them, mind. When the time comes, you'll load them into the boat, the one that puts me ashore behind Breakup Island.'

'How are you going to hump 'em once you reach the mainland?'

Jesson said shorly, 'I'll see about that when the time comes. Now go and get the gear.'

Bullock left the cabin, closing the door behind him. The bags were heavy; Jesson was going to have a hard task, and for a long way at that. His likely solution had not been lost on Bullock:

Jesson had ideas of forcing him along as well; or maybe he would come up with a promise of a split of the diamonds. Bullock had already given that possibility thought and he didn't go much on it. Too risky to his own life, and Jesson wouldn't prove trustworthy. But he was going to have to play along unless a miracle happened. Bullock sweated with more than the job of carrying the bags to Jesson; he fully realized that he was between the devil and the deep blue sea. If Jesson didn't knife him in the back once his usefulness ashore was over, then McRafferty was going to send in his report on arrival in Sydney. Bullock felt a shake in his hands and the start of real panic in his head. A choice was going to have to be made pretty soon now. Ashore, he would have a fighting chance. It would be a simple case of one man against the other; and come to that, Bullock still had his revolver, which Jesson didn't know about any more than McRafferty did.

The diamond bags transferred, Bullock went to his cabin to get the revolver.

* * *

'I'd give much to know what von Merkatz is up to,' Halfhyde said. Reports from the masthead lookout had indicated that the *Aysgarth Falls*, now identified as such by Halfhyde himself, who had gone aloft with a telescope, was still coming on under full sail for Breakup Island.

Graves said, 'I don't doubt we can expect him to weigh and steam south to lie off outside the Passage.'

'There's been no apparent reaction to him from the *Aysgarth Falls*,' Halfhyde pointed out. He brooded, feeling savage. It might not be long before the German warship's fighting top was sighted even if she didn't steam out from the lee of Breakup Island; and when von Merkatz in his turn sighted another ship entering such desolate and unlikely waters, then he *might* smell a very large rat and see some connection with Lieutenant Halfhyde. If he acted in some as yet unknown fashion upon his suspicions, all kinds of trouble might ensue and it was only too likely that Jesson would get away in the confusion. Besides,

155

Halfhyde, who disliked inactivity, was beginning to feel like a rat himself, one caught in a closing trap. His whole instinct was to force the issue now before it was too late; and he decided to act on that instinct. He said, 'The time has come for something else, sir.'

Graves gave him an enquiring look.

'We must go to sea. We must intercept the *Aysgarth Falls* immediately. I am sorry to sound peremptory and demanding, sir. But I have a duty to Captain McRafferty – and to the crown as well.'

'I gave you my promise of assistance,' Graves said mildly.

'Yes, sir. And I said I was grateful – I am. When we intercept the *Aysgarth Falls* I shall remove Jesson from the ship and bring him aboard you, relying once again on the effectiveness of the White Ensign against Admiral von Merkatz. Will you support me in that, sir?'

Graves nodded. 'I don't go back on my word, Halfhyde. You'll have my full support in anything you find necessary.'

'Thank you, sir. I ask the loan of a revolver, and the availability of a boat's crew for boarding.'

'And you shall have hands to board with you.'

Within the next five minutes the *Tacoma* had way upon her; with her paddles chunking through the water she headed for the open Pacific seaward of Disaster Passage, with a boat ready at the davits, swung out for lowering and manned by a crew picked from among the hardest cases aboard.

* * *

'A bloody steamer,' Bullock said. He spoke vindictively: the steamer had come out from a point southerly of Breakup Island and looked set to cross the windjammer's course inwards. The First Mate stared across the dismal grey of the sea as the sails, filled with a fair wind, carried the ship on towards the landing point. He gnawed at his lip, wondering if he should go below and tell Jesson; but decided not to. This wasn't Jesson's business and the man would only make difficulties, unnecessary ones. But the paddler was steering a dangerous

156

course; one that was not so far off a collision course, in fact. McRafferty was worried now. 'Blasted idiot!' he said. 'There's not a damned sailorman amongst the lot of them, in steam!' He watched the oncoming steamer closely, assessing her course which looked the more threatening as she came nearer. He shook with anger; the steamer had a lunatic in command. He shouted, 'Mr Bullock, all hands at once, man the braces . . . stand by to go about!'

Bullock, who was studying the steamer in increasing concern, didn't respond to the Captain's order. McRafferty repeated it, taking the First Mate by the shoulder and wrenching him round to face him. Bullock said harshly, 'Go about, my backside! We hold our course. She's crossing us clear and she's altering to starboard! I reckon she's going to come down our side – didn't you see —' He broke off in mid sentence, pushed McRafferty aside, and slid fast down the poop ladder to run along the waist, shouting for the hands. McRafferty, staring towards the steamer, now close and moving round his stern to come up on the port side, saw men mustered on her starboard paddle box.

One of them waved a hand and it was then that McRafferty recognized Halfhyde. His first reaction was one of sheer disbelief. After that, he moved fast. As he left the poop, Jesson emerged from the saloon hatch, his revolver in his hand.

* * *

Halfhyde stared across at the *Aysgarth Falls* as the *Tacoma* came round the stern of the windjammer, edging up to lie amidships for the jump across the gap. He had decided to board in naval fashion; he regretted only that the days of cutlasses were past. The manoeuvre would stand a better chance of success than any attempt to board from a boat; and Graves had agreed. Now Graves was handling his unwieldy ship superbly, watching with close attention as the starboard paddle moved closer to the side of the *Aysgarth Falls*, ready on the instant to go astern to bring the ship up when she was in position. Halfhyde watched Bullock. The First Mate was red-eyed with fear and fury as he stood waiting with the hands. Halfhyde wondered who would be for Bullock, who would be for McRafferty and himself. He saw McRafferty leave the poop and run for'ard, heard him shout out to Bullock and the hands. Bullock turned, his face vicious, and grappled with the Captain. McRafferty went down, but was soon on his feet again, having rolled his heavy body aside as Bullock lashed out at him with a booted foot. He rushed at Bullock, but the First Mate side-stepped and McRafferty lost his balance and went down again. As the steamer came closer in, Halfhyde, ready to jump across with half-a-dozen seamen, saw Float's friend Althwaite moving into the attack on McRafferty. It looked like wholesale mutiny now.

Halfhyde called, 'Ready?'

'All ready, sir.' This was the *Tacoma*'s bosun, who spat on his hands in anticipation.

'*Jump!*' Halfhyde roared.

There was something like a six-foot gap, with water slapping up as the hulls of the ships surged together. As the men cleared the gap, Graves took the *Tacoma* clear. Halfhyde was in the fight the moment he landed lightly on the deck. Bullock made a rush for him, but hadn't reckoned on Finney. The old ex-naval seaman knew well enough where his loyalties lay. He moved swiftly, stuck out a foot. Bullock crashed headlong on the deck, face first, his revolver spinning away into the scuppers. He got up, chin streaming blood from a nasty graze, and came back to the attack.

He checked himself when he saw Halfhyde's revolver. He stared around, looking for his own gun. Halfhyde said, 'Leave it, Bullock. Hands above your head. Any other movement and I'll fire.'

'You . . . bastard!'

Halfhyde grinned. The fighting was going on all around him, and it was about evens so far. A number of men were down on the deck and unconscious from fists and the swipe of belaying-pins. Halfhyde kept his revolver aimed at Bullock, moving closer to the First Mate, whose face was sheer murder now. He said, 'Aft, Bullock. Aft to the poop. Move!' Bullock stayed where he was; Halfhyde's long jaw came forward and he fired at the deck at Bullock's feet, his eyes like ice. Bullock yelped and moved fast. He climbed to the poop with Halfhyde close behind.

'Now,' Halfhyde said, swinging the First Mate round. 'Where's Sergeant Cantlow, Bullock?'

'Cantlow? I've never —'

'Cut the lies, Bullock. We both know the identity of your passenger. We also know what he's involved in – don't we? I advise you not to make matters worse for yourself. Where is he?'

Bullock's expression altered. Halfhyde recognized the purport too late. He was on the turn when from behind him a voice said, 'Here.' Halfhyde felt the pressure of metal in his spine. The voice said, 'Drop your revolver, friend. On the deck, behind you.'

Halfhyde looked back to meet Cantlow's eyes. 'A renegade sergeant of dragoons. Is there anything lower a man can do, than desert? Unless, of course, it's to commit murder. I suggest you think very carefully as to your next step, Sergeant Cantlow.'

Cantlow spoke over Halfhyde's shoulder to Bullock. 'Who is this man?'

'Halfhyde. I told you about him.'

'Yes, you did. Ex-Royal Navy, eh —'

'Not ex,' Halfhyde said. 'I am a lieutenant of Her Majesty's fleet still, though on the half-pay list. I am still the holder of Her Majesty's commission. It would be unwise to extend your felonies too far, Sergeant!'

Cantlow grinned; Halfhyde smelled whisky on his breath. 'I think you're in no position to give orders now, Lieutenant Halfhyde.'

'You think not?' Halfhyde lifted an arm and pointed across the water towards the *Tacoma*, now lying off at a safe distance. 'You see my ship. Take a good look, Sergeant Cantlow . . . and then tell me whether or not she wears the White Ensign of a Queen's ship!'

There was a pause. Behind Halfhyde, Cantlow swore viciously. He said, 'I'll be damned!'

'Exactly,' Halfhyde said. 'You'd do better to throw down your own revolver, Sergeant, than to interfere with mine.'

'Like hell. That ship . . . there's nothing she can do.' Once again Cantlow paused, then asked, 'What orders did you leave with her, before you boarded?'

Halfhyde shrugged. A bizarre idea was taking shape in his mind as a possibility, an audacious one that stood a fair chance, in his view, of paying off. Meanwhile it would be as well if Cantlow was left with the possibility of action by Graves. He said, 'You must use your imagination as to my orders, Sergeant —'

'No. You'll tell me, or it'll go the worse for you. In the meantime, you're going below to the saloon.' As Bullock picked up a belaying-pin Cantlow pressed with his gun. 'Down the hatch, Lieutenant Halfhyde, and make it fast or my temper may get the better of me. And hand me your revolver. Butt first.'

Halfhyde gave a shrug, passed the revolver over and turned for the hatch; for now, the physical odds were against him. Before reaching the hatch, he looked for'ard along the deck. The fo'c'sle hands of the *Aysgarth Falls* appeared to have won the day. The men from the *Tacoma* were mostly lying in pools of blood, and Captain McRafferty was being frog-marched aft towards the door into the saloon alleyway and looking the worse for wear. Matters were not good; and Halfhyde's request to Graves had been to take the *Tacoma* clear, to remain in company but not on any account to hazard his ship or the rest of his crew by making any further attempt to put a party aboard. The show was Halfhyde's; and it seemed now as though he might have been too confident. With no certain support arranged from the *Tacoma*, the future had to depend on what was, in fact, nothing but a very large bluff.

When Halfhyde reached the saloon, with Bullock in front of him and Cantlow bringing up the rear, McRafferty was sitting on the settee under guard of Althwaite and another man. Cantlow sent these two packing and ordered Halfhyde to the settee, where he sat alongside McRafferty, who was slumped with his head almost between his knees; the Master's face was

160

grey and drawn. There was a lump on his head and blood smeared his face. Halfhyde crossed his legs and assumed a relaxed air, a smile playing about his lips. McRafferty lifted his head and said in a dull voice, 'My ship. She'll be standing into danger . . . with no one on the poop.'

Cantlow caught Bullock's eye and nodded. He said, 'I'll be all right on my own, but listen out.' Bullock left the saloon and was heard clumping up the ladder to the poop. Cantlow addressed Halfhyde. 'You knew where we were heading – that's obvious. You knew just where to lie in wait for us, didn't you?'

'Certainly.'

'How? How did you know? And how did you know who I was?'

Halfhyde shrugged. There was no need to mention Float, who was still aboard the *Tacoma* and might yet be useful if held in reserve. He gave Cantlow part of the answer. He said, 'Sources in Chile.'

'What sources?'

Smiling still, Halfhyde said, 'Persons whom you thought were friends. In Iquique.' He added, 'It doesn't matter telling you that now, since you'll never be in a position to take your revenge. You're going to swing, Cantlow.'

Cantlow gave a coarse laugh. 'Doesn't look much like it, does it, Lieutenant Halfhyde? It doesn't look like it at all to my way of thinking.' He stood with his revolver pointed, his finger gently around the trigger, as the ship heeled to the wind and the sound of gear being worked came from the deck. 'What makes you so bloody confident? I'd just like to know.'

'You will know soon,' Halfhyde answered coolly.

Cantlow seemed baffled, looking as though a worm of worry was beginning to niggle. Halfhyde kept his easy air. Alongside him McRafferty's limbs had a nasty shake. He was seeing his whole life in ruins. As for the time being a silence fell on the saloon, McRafferty muttered that his daughter was being held in her cabin.

Halfhyde said, 'Not for much longer, Captain McRafferty.'

McRafferty looked up. 'How's that?'

'Time will tell, sir, as it will tell Sergeant Cantlow.'

'Cantlow . . .' McRafferty, Halfhyde had noted, had looked genuinely surprised when the name Cantlow had been mentioned a few moments earlier; and Halfhyde was convinced that McRafferty had never been told the true facts about his passenger. Now McRafferty put his head in his hands, a beaten man. Cantlow began to ask questions again, more insistent questions as to Halfhyde's sources of information, how he had managed to keep track of the *Aysgarth Falls* and how much was known in Chile and elsewhere as to himself. Halfhyde maintained his relaxed air, answering nothing except to say, repetitiously, that Cantlow would soon be finding out.

'You sound too damn confident,' Cantlow said furiously, coming closer with his revolver still pointed. 'If you don't want to get hurt, you'd better tell me what your confidence is based on, Lieutenant Halfhyde. All right?'

Halfhyde grinned into the lowering, hairy face. 'All in good time,' he said. At that moment something seemed to happen on deck. There was a shout from Bullock, a shout of fear and anger, followed by a spate of orders. In the saloon, they heard the thump of blocks and the sound of running feet; and then Bullock was heard coming down the ladder.

The First Mate burst into the saloon, eyes wide. He said, 'There's a bloody warship lying off Breakup Island! A bloody man-o'war, Cantlow!'

Cantlow's eyes had narrowed to slits and behind the beard the cheeks were suddenly pasty. He reached out and hauled Halfhyde to his feet. 'Is this why? Is this why you've been so damn confident?'

'Of course,' Halfhyde said. 'You're sailing to certain arrest, Sergeant. If Bullock looks carefully, he'll see the ensign of the German Empire . . . the ship is the first-class cruiser *Mannheim*, flagship of the German Special Service Squadron. Good friends . . . you'll not be forgetful that the Kaiser is the grandson of Her Majesty, of course —'

'You —'

Halfhyde's voice rose over the interruption. 'The squadron is commanded by my friend Vice-Admiral Paulus von Merkatz, who has placed himself at the disposal of the British Admiralty and of myself in particular – in order to arrest you, Sergeant Cantlow. You are sailing into his hands, and it's now too late.'

'It's never too late —'

'Ah, but it is this time.' Halfhyde waved a hand towards the saloon ports. 'Heavy guns, turreted guns – and upwards of five hundred naval officers and ratings. It will be an uphill task to take issue with them, Sergeant Cantlow. Frankly, I advise surrender.' He caught Bullock's eye and grinned. 'What do you say, Mr Bullock? Do you want to risk everything – or do you not?'

Bullock licked his lips, his eyes furtive now. He looked appealingly at Cantlow. Cantlow read the signs all too plainly: he was being walked out on. His face suffused and before Halfhyde could stop him he had fired. His aim was good. As Halfhyde took him hard with a blow behind the right ear, Bullock fell to the deck, streaming blood from his stomach.

* * *

Halfhyde paced the poop with McRafferty, who was all smiles now and feeling fit to resume the command of his ship. Cantlow was in irons below; Miss McRafferty stood at the starboard rail of the poop, letting the good, clean wind blow away the memories of the last few days. The *Tacoma*, after an exchange by megaphone with Halfhyde and McRafferty, had swung away on course for Sydney; and the *Aysgarth Falls* was now on a similar track, with Halfhyde promoted yet again, this time to First Mate.

'What about the diamonds, Mr Halfhyde?' McRafferty asked.

'I've examined the cases, sir, and they appear to be intact. They can be safely delivered to the proper authority in Sydney.'

'Yes. But do you suppose the recovery of them will act in my favour, enough to prevent charges against me?'

'I'd not be surprised,' Halfhyde answered. 'Also, I shall stand by you myself and confirm my own belief that you had no knowledge of Cantlow's identity or of what was in his baggage.'

163

'Very good of you.' McRafferty mopped at his face, looking much relieved.

Halfhyde shrugged. 'I've no wish to see a shipowner suffer unjustly – I'm still hopeful of becoming an owner myself and I've already seen some of the difficulties involved! Further, Bullock and Cantlow were villains both, and I see no justice whatever in allowing their villainy to stick to you.'

McRafferty nodded. 'I'm very grateful, Mr Halfhyde. My ship . . . as you know, it's my home.' He blew his nose hard; he seemed embarrassed and to cover this he lifted his telescope towards the German flagship still lying off Breakup Island and now beginning to recede astern as the windjammer made all speed for Sydney Heads. 'Your friend, Mr Halfhyde.'

'Friend?' Halfhyde asked absently.

'The Admiral – von Merkatz I think you said —'

'Ah, yes. What about him, sir?'

'You wish to make no farewell message, perhaps by sema-phore, before we're too far south of him? A message of thanks? It seems —'

Halfhyde said gravely, 'I doubt if he would really appreciate it, sir.'

'But surely —'

'No, sir. I shall refrain from rubbing in the salt on this occasion.'

'Salt? Why, damn it, Mr Halfhyde, I fail to understand you! The German's been of immense help and you don't even thank him – and then you talk of salt!'

Halfhyde tapped McRafferty's telescope, which he had now lowered. He said, 'Look again, sir, and carefully. I think your seamanship sense would have told you earlier, had you not been somewhat *distrait*. I believe Bullock – fortunately – was also *distrait* at the moment of sighting her.' He coughed and said again, 'Another look, Captain.'

Still puzzled, McRafferty lifted his glass and steadied it against the mizzen shrouds. He stared for some while towards the flagship. 'There's a good deal of activity around her,' he said. He looked a while longer then said in amazement, 'Why, the poor fellow's hard aground, Mr Halfhyde, hard aground on

164

the rocks!'

Halfhyde smiled. 'Indeed he is. He impacted sharply in the very moment of coming out from the lee of Breakup Island.' His smile became broader as he reflected upon the wrath that would visit von Merkatz if ever he found out about his unwitting assistance to his old enemy. 'The very best place for him, sir,' he added to McRafferty.

'But that cannot be – we must go back to assist —'

'No, sir.' Halfhyde was adamant. 'We must not go about. For certain good reasons, it's a far better thing to let grounded Huns lie.'